# "Grace, you're obviously the perfect assistant to be lost with in the outback."

Grace looked at her hand, which had practically disappeared inside his strong grasp. "If only I was also willing," she muttered, snatching her hand away. And then she grimaced. He'd caught her off guard and now she'd let fly with a hopelessly stupid remark.

"Willing?" Mitch remained standing directly in front of her, a perplexed expression in his eyes.

"Please, forget I said that."

He smiled and brushed the hair back from her cheek. "A wild and willing Grace would be an unexpected bonus." Then his face grew serious again. "But it won't get us o___ ___"

**Barbara Hannay** was born in Sydney, Australia, educated in Brisbane and spent most of her adult life living in tropical north Queensland, where she and her husband have raised four children. While she has enjoyed many happy times camping and canoeing in the bush, she also delights in an urban lifestyle—chamber music, contemporary dance, movies and dining out. An English teacher, she has always loved writing, and now, by having her stories published, she is living her most cherished fantasy.

## Books by Barbara Hannay

# OUTBACK WITH THE BOSS

*Barbara Hannay*

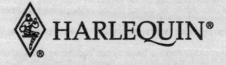

TORONTO • NEW YORK • LONDON
AMSTERDAM • PARIS • SYDNEY • HAMBURG
STOCKHOLM • ATHENS • TOKYO • MILAN • MADRID
PRAGUE • WARSAW • BUDAPEST • AUCKLAND

ISBN 0-373-03670-1

OUTBACK WITH THE BOSS

First North American Publication 2001.

Copyright © 2000 by Barbara Hannay.

This edition published by arrangement with Harlequin Books S.A.

® and TM are trademarks of the publisher. Trademarks indicated with ® are registered in the United States Patent and Trademark Office, the Canadian Trade Marks Office and in other countries.

Visit us at www.eHarlequin.com

Printed in U.S.A.

# CHAPTER ONE

GRACE ROBBINS reached into her carryall and reluctantly drew out her black lace lingerie. Nervously, her fingers traced the delicate ribbon trim while she wondered how on earth she could go ahead with Maria's outrageous suggestion. Until now, she'd only ever worn these revealing garments under her faithful 'little black dress'. She'd *never* considered displaying her low-cut underwired bra and high-cut wispy knickers on their own.

'The problem is you're a natural prude,' Grace told her reflection in the mirror. She didn't enjoy parading in front of a man. Wearing a bikini on the beach was bad enough.

She sighed. Perhaps the solution was to take this one step at a time. She'd already let herself into her boyfriend's flat. If she put the underwear on beneath her other clothes for now, she could decide whether to go ahead with the rest of her friend's crazy plan later.

Halfway through this process, Grace paused and studied her image in the full-length mirror. The dramatic effect of her body, framed by a doorway and encased in nothing but skimpy, sensuous black lace, was surprising. Maria was probably right. It would take Henry by surprise too.

But how on earth could she carry this off? And if she did, what could she possibly say to justify such madness?

She sent the mirror a grimacing grin and tried striking a sexy pose, announcing to the empty room, 'Ta-da! National Underwear Display Day!'

No, she thought with a shudder. She looked and sounded ridiculous.

She tried another, more demure pose. 'I'll show you mine, if you show me yours?' *Definitely not.*

Oh, heavens, thought Grace, why am I even bothering? This just isn't me. Bringing her hands to her face in mock horror, she tried one more time. 'Henry, the little black dress thieves have struck and left me with nothing to wear!'

Groaning, she decided it was absolutely no use. Playing *femme fatale* was definitely not her scene. She couldn't ever make this work.

Grace glanced at the clock on the dressing table and decided there was no need to panic just yet. She still had at least an hour before Henry would return. She had to think this through calmly and rationally.

She grimaced. *Calmly and rationally?* She hadn't been able to place one logical thought next to another for days. Her fists clenched. *It was all Mitch Wentworth's fault!* The new boss had forced her into this pickle!

For the past fortnight, just thinking about Mitch Wentworth's arrival to take over the company had seemed to banish every composed and sane idea from Grace's usually clear-thinking head. And it was her fuming and fretting about this man that had launched Maria's lame-brained idea in the first place.

The whole wild plan had started at lunchtime when Maria had rested her plump elbows on the cafeteria table, and leaned towards Grace with her best lecturing expression. 'For goodness' sake,' she'd sighed. 'Stop stewing about Mitch Wentworth and concentrate on the bonuses. *Our new boss is a stud!* He's flying in to take over Tropicana Films any day now, and as you're his assistant you get to work side by side with him. Did you see his photo on the cover of *Movie Mag*?'

Out of her voluminous handbag, Maria had dragged a

glossy magazine and tossed it onto the red laminated tabletop.

'Of course I've seen it,' Grace had retorted, her nose crinkling in disgust. 'I took one look at his self-satisfied smirk and the bimbos hanging off each arm and wanted to hand in my resignation, pronto.'

'Self-satisfied smirk?' Maria's dark eyes twinkled with tolerant disbelief. 'Come on, that's a really cute smile in anyone's books. Mitch is the ultimate in T. D. and H.'

'Pardon?'

'Tall, dark and hard to get.'

Grace's lips had pursed into a tight circle as she'd pushed the magazine aside. 'I'm sure, in *his* case, it'll be tall, dark and hard to please. Working for him will be awful.'

Maria threw her arms in the air. 'Half the women in the movie industry would be lining up for your job just to breathe the same air as Mitch Wentworth.'

'That's enough!' Grace moaned. 'All I hear about from Henry is how lucky I am to be working for the great Mitch Wentworth.'

'Henry?' Maria clicked her fingers in triumph. 'Now I get it! It's not Wentworth who's your problem. It's the boyfriend, Henry. I should have guessed.'

Grace rolled her eyes. 'I made the mistake of outlining the plot of Wentworth's next movie *New Tomorrow* and now Henry spends every night designing fancy computer graphics he's absolutely convinced Wentworth will want to use.'

'So he doesn't have any time for you?'

'Exactly,' Grace snapped.

She'd met Henry soon after arriving in Townsville from Sydney and it had been good to have someone to show her around. But over the past fortnight, as his obsession with impressing her new boss had gained momentum, her enthusiasm for him had diminished rather rapidly.

Grace's track record with men made her extra wary. She was still plagued by memories of Roger the Rat, a supersuave mover and shaker, who'd broken her heart. After that shattering experience, it hadn't taken long to convince her that the business world was a breeding ground for men who were superficially quite gorgeous, but so full of their own egos, they trampled all over women and usually left them feeling used and abused.

That was why she'd dated Henry. He wasn't handsome, but he had other virtues Grace preferred these days. He was scholarly and serious and, most importantly, safe.

She'd shrugged. 'I—I don't think it's that Henry's not interested. It's just that he gets kind of…distracted.'

A disgusted grunt had prefaced Maria's response. 'Distracted? What can divert a real man from your long legs and green eyes, not to mention the bits in between?'

Grace let out a short, self-conscious laugh. 'Computers are very fascinating toys.'

With a groan, Maria threw her head back and had stared at the cafeteria's ceiling. Then she had slowly lowered her gaze. 'You two are getting physical, aren't you?'

Feeling distinctly uneasy, Grace ran nervous fingers through her thick tawny hair, flicking it away from her collar. 'We will—I'm sure. I feel quite—er—fond of Henry. It's—it's all a matter of—timing.'

'Timing?' Maria almost shrieked. She shook her head in dismay. 'My dear girl, the answer's clear-cut. You forget about Henry and set your sights higher.'

'Higher? How much higher? What do you mean?'

'Mitch Wentworth, of course. You could snaffle the new boss. You've certainly got everything it takes.' Maria had looked down at her own chubby figure and groaned. 'If only I didn't love chocolate.'

Grace jumped to her feet. 'The new boss? For crying out loud, Maria, where's your loyalty? Think what he's done to our old boss, George Hervey. The poor old fellow's been tossed on the scrap heap by this take-over. Wentworth just blasted his way into Tropicana Films and we're expected to whip straight into "Yes, sir. No, sir".'

She sat down again and reached for her friend's hand. 'Thanks for the sympathetic ear, but you're way off beam. I can't stand the idea of even working for the man, let alone...' Her mind had darted frantically away from the mere thought of making a play for her boss. She slumped back into her chair. 'I'll definitely stick with Henry.'

'You're sure?'

Suddenly Grace had been very sure.

Having a boyfriend like Henry was sensible and safe—like wearing a seat belt in a car. But giving a bully-boy showman like Mitch Wentworth so much as a second glance was as wise as skinny-dipping with sharks. 'I've just got to find some way to get Henry away from his computer and interested in me again.'

Maria's face was split by a sudden grin. 'Don't worry, my dear. I can feel a bright idea coming on. We'll put an end to this nonsense of Henry's. Tonight's the night. Before our Mr. Wentworth gets here to totally distract your boyfriend, we'll *undistract* him. We'll *make* Henry notice you!'

'Oh, I don't know if that's necessary.' Maria had started to get just a touch too pushy. How had one little gripe about Mitch Wentworth escalated to the point where her friend had been about to launch a rescue mission on her love life?

'I appreciate your good intentions,' she'd hedged, disliking the hard edge in her tone, but too tense to do anything about it. 'But I'm not quite dateless and desperate. And I really think this is just between Henry and me.'

Grace's glance fell to Mitch Wentworth's grinning face on the cover of *Movie Mag* and an image of him standing in her office had floated dangerously into her thoughts. Once her new boss arrived, that cheeky smile, those naughty-boy eyes and those highly indecent muscles would be mere inches away from her.

Maria eyed her shrewdly and Grace had the terrible feeling that the other woman knew exactly what was bugging her! How on earth could she carry on with her work each day while a man like Mitch Wentworth flaunted his lethal, sexy weapons around her office?

He hadn't even arrived yet and already her thoughts had been trailing in his direction like ants to a picnic basket.

That shocking realisation had prompted Grace into action. 'Okay, you win,' she'd told Maria. 'I'll give Henry one last chance. What's your brilliant idea?'

But listening to Maria's action plan had been the easy part.

Now, as Grace stood eyeing her reflection in Henry's mirror, the sight of her wide, anxious eyes and her nervous, fiddling fingers reminded her that she wasn't really up to the task ahead.

She could deal with the twinge of guilt she felt about leaving work early and letting herself into Henry's flat. The missed time could be made up on another day.

But she couldn't face the final step.

This mission was impossible. There was no way she could pose at Henry's front door and carry out the rest of the plan.

The sense of elation Mitch Wentworth had hoped for when he'd arrived in Townsville was somehow evading him. It must be jet lag, he told himself as he ran a weary hand over his eyes. A flight from San Francisco with only a few hours' stopover in his home town, Sydney, before heading north to Townsville would knock the stuffing out of most travellers. And it was probably a mistake to take a peek at his brand-new baby—the Tropicana Films studios—unannounced and so late in the day.

At this stage, there was only an advance team working on the project, so he'd expected half the offices to be empty. And it *was* six-thirty in the evening, so it was not surprising that all his employees had gone home.

Even the formidable Ms Robbins.

Her name was on the door of the office in front of him. Grace Robbins. After all George Hervey had told him about this woman's efficiency, dedication to the company and amazingly wide range of skills, he thought that perhaps— just *perhaps*—she might have stayed behind to meet him. In fact, once he'd faxed her his flight times, he'd almost expected her to greet him at the airport.

As he'd made his way through the Townsville terminal, he had kept a weather eye out for a middle-aged woman, conservatively dressed, brandishing perhaps a clipboard or some other weapon of efficiency. That was how he pictured Grace Robbins after listening to George's twenty-minute eulogy of her.

Clearly George's praise had been way too enthusiastic and his claims too exaggerated. It was a regrettable oversight, Mitch decided as he moved into her office. He was going out on a financial limb with *New Tomorrow*. With almost all his own money invested in it, this movie had to be a resounding hit and he needed the best possible staff to support him. He expected Ms Robbins to be a key player in the project.

Shrugging aside his annoyance, Mitch tried to be reasonable. Perhaps he shouldn't judge the woman just because she wasn't still here when he crept into town virtually unannounced. He'd only sent the fax just before he left Sydney and she might have had an appointment—any number of reasons for rushing home.

His eyes scanned the office. He couldn't judge much at this stage. Her computer was shut down of course. There was a pile of faxes on her desk, but he had no intention of snooping. At least she wasn't someone who littered her desk with personal knick-knacks or family photographs. Mitch approved of that. He liked a staff who kept their business and personal lives completely separate.

His glance caught the latest copy of *Movie Mag* lying at the edge of her desk.

Frowning, Mitch picked it up. The frown deepened and his eyes narrowed. Someone had taken a thick black marker pen and added graffiti to the cover. His picture sported an Adolf Hitler-style moustache and enormous black-rimmed spectacles. Several of his teeth had been blackened, leaving him with a ludicrous, gap-toothed smile.

Mitch's shoulders rose, then slumped as he drew in a long breath before expelling it slowly in a hiss through his teeth. With slow, deliberate movements, he folded the offending magazine and placed it thoughtfully in his coat pocket.

And as he prowled back through the empty building he felt more jet-lagged than ever.

When he reached the thick glass doors at the entrance to the studio, a tall, dark shape outside caught his attention. An agitated young man was gesticulating wildly—pointing to himself and then to Mitch. For a moment, Mitch experienced a surge of hope. Had one eager employee returned to greet him? But just as quickly he dismissed the fanciful notion. Anyone working for the company would be able to let himself in.

Mitch opened the door and the fellow launched forward, his hand outstretched.

'Mr Wentworth?'

Mitch nodded as the man stepped through the doorway and he shook the proffered hand. 'How do you do?'

'Henry Aspinall. And I'm very well, sir. I must say this is indeed a great honour. Oh, boy, it's such a stroke of luck meeting you here, Mr Wentworth, sir. I've been trying to ring Grace all afternoon to check your arrival time and...'

Mitch interrupted the enthusiastic outburst. 'Grace? Grace Robbins? You know her?'

'Sure.' Henry nodded. 'When I couldn't reach her at her flat, I thought she must still be here.'

'No, there's no one here—not even Ms Robbins,' Mitch confirmed.

'Oh, well, not to worry.' Henry grinned. 'It was really you I wanted to meet. You've received my e-mail messages?'

Mitch rubbed his brow, cursing the tiredness that fogged his memory. 'Aspinall, Aspinall...' He needed to recall whether this was someone really important he should remember, or just a nuisance fan.

Henry took advantage of the hesitation. 'Grace told me about *New Tomorrow* and I've designed some computer graphics to blend in beautifully with the North Queensland outback...'

Mitch held up his hand to halt the flow of Henry's enthusiasm. 'Of course. You swamped my Los Angeles office with messages. You've done some graphics for the battle scenes.'

Henry looked jubilant. 'That's it, sir! What do you think? Would you like to see them?'

Mitch shot Henry an appraising glance. 'Do you mind if we start walking? I'd kinda like to get to my hotel.'

'Yes, sir. No problem. Where are you staying? The Sheraton? I'd be honoured to give you a lift.'

Mitch shrugged. Why not go with the fellow? It would save hunting up another taxi. While under other circumstances he might have found Henry Aspinall's zeal annoying, like the unwanted attentions of an over-enthusiastic puppy, this evening it appealed to his dented ego. At least someone was keen to see him and seemed eager for his film's success. He grunted his acceptance of the offer.

As they stepped onto the street, Henry skipped along the pavement with excitement. 'My flat's on the way. I've got everything set up. We could call in and I could quickly show you—'

Mitch held up his hand and nodded. 'Sure thing,' he agreed as Henry opened the passenger door of a battered and rusty sedan. 'Take me to your disk.'

To his relief, they pulled up in front of a set of low maisonettes within five minutes. The car door squeaked on its hinges as Mitch prepared to follow Henry into his flat. After sitting for even such a short time, his weariness had returned with a vengeance. He would make this call as brief as possible. All he wanted now was to crawl into crisp, clean hotel sheets and sleep for three days.

'That's funny,' commented Henry as they crossed the short strip of weedy front lawn. 'I don't remember leaving any lights on.' He shrugged a puzzled smile Mitch's way before sorting through his keys for the one he needed.

But his key never reached the lock.

As their footsteps echoed on the concrete paving of the narrow entryway, the front door flew open.

'Surprise!'

A blaze of light flooded the doorway, illuminating a

beautiful creature wearing next to nothing. Her eyes were fixed on Henry.

'It's Tuesday! National Girlfriend Exposure Day!'

Standing back in the shadows, Mitch was vaguely aware of strangling noises coming from Henry, but he was too stunned to move or speak.

A goddess, tall and tawny-headed, posed before them, dressed in the briefest of black lacy undergarments. She was absolutely breathtaking. Her creamy skin was satin-smooth and her womanly curves perfectly shaped—delicate slenderness and lush fullness balanced in proportions designed to impel a man to reach out for them.

He blinked, but shot his eyes wide open again in case he missed something.

And what he noticed was the 'something' in her eyes that didn't quite mesh with this vision of alluring temptress. Was it fear, embarrassment? The shy tilt of her head and the downward curve of her shoulders made him think of a little girl pushed into the stage's limelight by an overly ambitious parent. This woman had the body of a sultry seductress and the mien of a vulnerable child.

'What on earth are you doing?' Henry yelled.

His voice sent her slumping against the door frame like a puppet whose strings had been cut. But, almost instantly, her eyes flew to Mitch and she suddenly jerked again to terrified life.

'Oh, my gosh,' she moaned, and stared at Mitch in absolute horror. She clasped her hands to her chest. 'Oh, no! *Oh, no!*' she cried.

Her arm shot out and the door slammed in their faces.

# CHAPTER TWO

'GRACE! What *has* got into you?'

Grace turned, shaking with terror, her eyes wide and her hand covering her mouth, as she watched Henry stride across his living room towards her. His crimson face was twisted with anger.

'Do you realise what you've just done?' he shouted. 'Do you know who—?' Henry stopped shouting abruptly, as if he realised he was making this fiasco much worse. His voice dropped to a panicky whisper. 'That's Mitch Wentworth at the door!'

'I know, I know,' Grace moaned. Her eyes hunted around the small room, searching frantically for any item of clothing she could grab. Where was a gaping black hole when she needed to leap into it?

'How could you do this to me, Grace? What's he going to think?'

As if the answer to his own question suddenly popped into his head, Henry swore, spun on his heel and darted back to his front door.

Grace made a speedy escape to the bedroom.

'He's gone!' she heard Henry roar. 'Wentworth's left already!'

She sank with relief onto the bed. Thank heavens for that. With shaking hands, she pulled a T-shirt over her head.

Henry burst into the room. 'You've ruined me! You do realise that, don't you? I'll never get Wentworth to look at my graphics now.' Flinging his hands into the air, he glared

16

at her. 'I had Mitch Wentworth here, Grace. Here in my own home. He was going to look at all my designs tonight! Tonight! You stupid woman! You've spoilt everything.'

Grace shuddered. 'I'm sorry, Henry,' she replied dully. 'How was I to know you'd bring him home? I didn't even know the man was in Townsville.' With nervous, wrenching movements, she pulled on her jeans. All she could think of was how badly she wanted to get away.

And never come back!

Henry was carrying on like a spoilt little boy who'd dropped his ice-cream cone in the dirt.

'I'm sure you'll be able to show your ideas to him some other time,' she muttered. Why had she ever wasted one moment trying to arouse Henry's interest in her? He couldn't have been less appreciative of her efforts if she'd trashed his entire flat.

She shoved her feet into trainers. 'I'm sorry my silly plan was such a flop,' she told him as he slumped and sulked on the far side of the bed. Her shoulders rose in a dismissive shrug. 'It—it seemed like a good idea at the time...'

But not any more! A wave of shame drenched her with fresh horror. Never had she been more aware of being in the wrong place at the wrong time.

Henry shook his head and growled. 'I thought you were supposed to be smart, but that was about the dumbest thing I've ever seen.'

One thing was for sure, Grace promised herself silently: Henry wouldn't see anything like that ever again. Jumping up, she grabbed her carryall and offered him a mumbled, 'I won't hang around,' before blinking back embarrassed tears, hurrying past him and out of the room.

But as she left his flat Grace winced at the thought of a much more pressing concern than Henry's fit of the sulks. Her big, bigger, *biggest* problem was so horrendous she wished she could take off on the next space shuttle! She'd gladly spend six months on a space station in the far reaches of the universe.

There was no way on earth she could face her new boss in the morning.

Please, please, *please* don't let him recognise me.

When Mitch Wentworth stepped into her office next morning, Grace huddled over her computer and prayed as she had never prayed before.

She was prepared to repent in sackcloth and ashes. She would make a big donation to charity. She could do both. Anything. Just as long as her boss didn't connect her with that humiliating moment in Henry's doorway.

This morning, she'd taken great pains to look as different from the previous night's pouting sexpot as she possibly could. But was it enough? Suddenly, with Mitch Wentworth's expensive, hand-stitched shoes firmly planted in the middle of her office, Grace doubted the ability of hair gel and a primly fashioned bun to effectively change her appearance. And how helpful were the heavily framed glasses she'd borrowed from her neighbour? Her only reassurance was that last night Mitch had glimpsed her very briefly. And surely the shapeless, dull brown dress disguised her body?

What had actually been said at Henry's front door was all an embarrassing blur, but with a hefty dollop of luck Mitch Wentworth would have no idea she was remotely connected to Henry Aspinall—or the trollop who'd greeted him last night.

Nevertheless, as he moved towards her, her shoulders lifted and squared as if she was braced to take a blow.

'Good morning. I presume I have the pleasure of meeting

Ms Robbins?' His dark eyes assessed her carefully, but they showed no sign of recognition.

*Yes!* Relief flowed and swirled through Grace, but she still couldn't dredge up a smile as she replied, 'Good morning, Mr Wentworth.' She stood and held out her hand to greet him formally, and the room buzzed with her tension. His handshake was predictably strong and firm.

My, he was tall! And broad-shouldered. She'd been prepared for the well-defined bone structure, the thick dark hair and the eyes designed purely for seduction, and last night she'd realised he was a big man. But now, in her small office, he took up far too much space. There was no escaping his spectacular style of masculinity: the kind of looks she'd learned to mistrust instinctively.

'You come highly recommended. George Hervey gave a glowing report.'

She smiled faintly.

Mitch did not smile back. 'But, of course, that's all over now. With me, you will have to prove yourself.'

*Prove myself?*

Despite her nervousness, a surge of defiance heated Grace's cheeks. *Here we go! The bloodthirsty pirate takes the helm!* Her chin lifted automatically, but, just in time, she remembered to mask her stormy reaction by lowering her gaze. Her green eyes had a bad habit of attracting unwanted attention when her dander was up. And already she could feel her hackles rising.

Mitch spoke again, his deep Australian drawl blending with the American twang he'd acquired after many years in the United States. 'I expect one hundred per cent commitment and loyalty.'

'Of course, Mr Wentworth.'

He drew in a sharp breath and Grace suspected that her softly spoken subservience irked him. Nevertheless, he con-

tinued without missing another beat. 'You're a vital key to
the success of this *New Tomorrow* project. But…' his voice
dropped and he paused for dramatic effect '…I *am* that
project. You're working for me now, Grace Robbins. When
you think of *New Tomorrow,* you think of me.'

He was as full of himself as she'd expected! However,
she couldn't ignore the fact that his brainchild was very
exciting—a project she itched to become more involved
with.

'Your film has a brilliant premise,' she replied, and
would have continued, but, with an ominous flourish, Mitch
reached into his pocket and withdrew something that
looked like a magazine.

He threw it onto the table.

Her boss grinned up at her, *his face disguised by a bristly
moustache.*

*Rimless spectacles.*

*And blackened teeth!*

Grace's stomach felt as if it had been pumped full of
concrete. Slashed onto the page with thick, black, angry
strokes, her graffiti was clear evidence of the tantrum she'd
thrown in this very office after her lunchtime discussion
with Maria.

*How on earth had he found it?*

She flinched.

And suppressed a whimper.

Gulped down the urge to scream. Why couldn't real life
be like making a movie? If only a director could jump into
her office and yell, 'Cut! I don't like the way this scene's
falling. Let's start again and *this* time we'll leave out the
magazine…'

But no.

No one was going to rescue her from her own reckless
actions. For several seconds Grace hoped she might faint.

No such luck.

Her legs trembled, but didn't give way. No comforting blackness descended. And Mitch Wentworth remained standing squarely in front of her, pinning her to the spot with his cold, unflinching stare.

'It seems you have a problem,' he challenged.

She swayed slightly and grasped the back of her chair.

'Obviously, you've got a problem with me,' Mitch repeated in a cold, flat voice.

Where had she heard that the best defence was to attack? With a shaking, accusing finger, she pointed at him. 'You— you've been spying on me!'

He stared at her in simmering silence. Then, to her surprise, he shook his head and walked away. For several seconds, Mitch stood with his back to her, but Grace could sense his anger in the rise and fall of his shoulders. He turned swiftly to face her again. 'I don't spy, Ms Robbins! I called here yesterday evening to check out the office. *My* office. And it didn't take the help of a special service investigator to uncover what you left lying so blatantly on your desk. Right here!'

Grace looked away. He was about to sack her. She knew it. And if she stretched her imagination to take in his point of view she probably couldn't blame him.

But she loved this job. Over the past four years, it had become the single most important thing in her life! Somehow, she dragged her eyes upwards again to find Mitch studying her. His hands were now shoved deep into his trouser pockets. If he was going to fire her, she wished he would get it over quickly.

'Do you want to see this project through?'

'Huh? I—I mean I beg your pardon?'

'*New Tomorrow.* You want to stay on the team?'

'Yes, I do. Very much. I'm actually very committed to *New Tomorrow*. I—'

'You want to work with me?'

For a fraction of a second she hesitated, but it was long enough to elicit another of his quick frowns.

'Yes. Yes, I do.'

Mitch picked up the offending magazine and tossed it into her waste-paper basket. Then he began to pace the small square of carpet in the middle of her office. 'Okay. We'll forget about this, Grace.'

*Grace?* He'd dropped the Ms Robbins?

'I don't have any problems at this stage,' he continued. 'If you have problems you should get them off your chest.' He shot a questioning glance her way.

She shook her head.

'You're quite sure?' he persisted.

Of course she had objections about Mitch Wentworth. She had a list as long as both his arms. But what could she do with them?

Especially now, when he'd skilfully backed her into a corner?

How could an employee criticise her boss for the way he'd bulldozed his way into taking over George Hervey's little film company? As for her other problems—there was no way she could lambaste a man for his killer good looks.

She really had no choice but to offer an olive branch. 'I have no complaints,' she told him. 'And—and I apologise. You were never meant to see the silly doodling on that magazine. I admit…I've been…rather thoughtless.'

He half turned and eyed her speculatively, his hands resting on his hips, pushing his suit coat aside. He was still too damned good-looking to be let loose in small spaces.

'But,' she finished defiantly, 'can you spare me another speech?'

He chuckled and, for the briefest of moments, his eyes danced before his frown slid quickly back into place. 'No, Grace, I'm afraid you'll have to bear with me for a little longer. You see, from now on, people will have to get used to following my orders. And the *New Tomorrow* project must dominate everybody's thinking. It's my single focus and it's got to be the focus for everyone else on the team. For anyone who's not on that wavelength, there's going to be a lot of pain and suffering. And if heads have to roll...' his own head cocked to one side and he glared at her '...then so be it.'

'I understand,' Grace responded, a little flush mounting on her cheeks. How dared he suggest she wasn't focused? She'd always taken great pride in her professional commitment. 'I'm quite well aware that I'm playing with the big boys now.'

Perhaps she had gone too far. Grace squirmed uneasily as Mitch's jaw clenched and his frown lingered while he studied her face. 'The big boys...' he repeated softly. His dark eyes linked for an uncomfortably long moment with hers. They moved to her mouth.

And Grace felt as if she'd stepped into quicksand.

How did he do it?

His hands were now lodged firmly in both trouser pockets and he was standing a good metre and a half away and yet, the way his eyes touched her—she felt as if his mouth was caressing hers—*intimately*.

This was ridiculous!

She tightened the lips he seemed to be studying so intently. And, her mind racing, she began to talk—anything to cover her turmoil. 'I—I think you'll find that I've been networking successfully on the location options, Mr Wentworth. I've already contacted the property owners in the Tablelands and Gulf regions. I've been inundated with

offers of accommodation from tourist operators in the
north. I have contour maps from the army, information on
the roads... The internet is invaluable...'

Mitch held up his hand. 'Hold it. Okay, I'm impressed,
but I don't need an itemised account just yet. I'm sure it's
all in your report.'

Her eyes blazed. 'How can I help babbling? You make
me nervous when you...when you keep *staring* at me...like
that.' A swift flood of heat rushed into her cheeks.

Mitch took a step closer and, for a breath-robbing moment, Grace thought he was going to touch her. 'You don't
like men looking at you?' he asked lazily.

'Of course I don't,' she snapped while her heart thun-
dered.

His eyes left her then, and he turned to the opposite wall,
but an annoying little smile tugged at the corner of his
mouth.

'No woman does!' she said indignantly. *What was so
darned amusing?*

'Ogling women is certainly inappropriate in the work-
place,' Mitch agreed, while he appeared to examine with
fascination a 'Save the Rainforest' poster on her wall. 'I
apologise if I seemed to be staring. You have an intriguing...face.'

Grace gulped, uncertain how to react.

He moved to the door then stopped. With his thumb,
Mitch traced the straight timber edge of the door frame.

Grace's heartbeats continued to trouble her. He hesitated
as if he still wanted to tick her off about something and
she wished he'd get it over and done with.

A dreadful thought struck and her hands clenched so
tightly her fingernails dug into her palms. *Surely he wasn't
about to announce that he'd recognised her after all? He
knew she was the hussy in the wispy triangles of black lace?*

*Not now?*

But when his eyes swung back to hers, although they glinted with secret amusement, he merely nodded his head and said with studied politeness, 'Nice to meet you, Grace. I'll look forward to reading your report.'

He turned and left and Grace's knees buckled. She sank onto a chair.

Groaning, she tried to reassure herself that Mitch couldn't have known about last night in Henry's flat. She was panicking about nothing. If he'd recognised her, he would have brought it out in the open—the way he had with the magazine.

*Yikes! The magazine!* With a moan of despair, she buried her face in her hands. *The magazine! The underwear!* How could she cope?

Staring through her fingers at her keyboard, Grace knew the full meaning of regret. But, she decided after a few minutes of blistering remorse, what she regretted most was that the human brain wasn't more like a computer. If only there was a safe way to wipe a man's memory...and get away with it.

# CHAPTER THREE

MITCH closed Grace's preliminary report on location options for *New Tomorrow* and placed it carefully on his desk. Leaning back in his chair, he glanced at his watch and stretched his arms above him. He was surprised that it was already seven p.m. No wonder his stomach was growling with hunger. In the past three days since he'd arrived in town, there'd been so much work to get through that he'd stayed back in the office each night, then grabbed a snack from the sandwich bar next door rather than eating properly in the hotel's restaurant.

He allowed his arms to drop again and inter-linked his hands behind his neck. It was his favourite position for thinking.

And he needed to think about Grace Robbins.

This report she'd submitted was impressive. The clear, concise writing, the maps and illustrations, the impeccable layout and thorough attention to detail showed beyond doubt that Grace was absolutely professional. She was one smooth operator.

In the two months since she'd moved from the Sydney office to be part of the advance team working out of Townsville, Grace had assimilated an amazing amount of information about the northern region and all of it was highly relevant to their project. While reading her report, Mitch had become excited by all the potential location sites she'd outlined.

What had really surprised him was her uncanny grasp of what he was trying to achieve with this movie. He'd only sent a fairly sketchy proposal; she hadn't even read a full script. But it was as if he and Grace had already shared several in-depth conversations about his hopes and expectations for *New Tomorrow.*

An assistant who could methodically work her way through extraneous details to find exactly what was relevant was a great asset. But one who could also share his artistic vision was a rare find. When her efficiency and presentation skills were also considered, Mitch knew George Hervey had been right. Grace was of inestimable value to the company.

It was a pity these qualities didn't come with a pleasant, sunny personality. There was only one way to describe Grace—well-balanced—with a huge chip on both shoulders!

Throughout the three days he'd spent in the office, her face had remained a polite, but frowning, almost unfriendly mask. And, while it didn't particularly bother him, Mitch was beginning to think he'd dreamed up that vision of an alluring, provocative beauty framed by the doorway of Henry Aspinall's flat.

The way she scurried around the office with her head down, dressed in sombre browns and greys, she looked like a drab brown mouse. It was hard to believe she'd ever made a sexy come-on in her life.

Perhaps he should have said something to clear the air. But he hadn't wanted any blurring of business and private matters between himself and the woman with whom he had to work so closely.

He flipped open the plastic cover of the report and turned again to Grace's recommendations. Pen in hand, he read through them once more, circling certain points and making notes in the margins. She had certainly presented some thought-provoking options.

*    *    *

Grace was in the mood for cooking something special. It was an inspiration that didn't hit her often, so she tended to make the most of it, preparing large quantities that would last her for many meals. Occasionally she felt expansive and threw a dinner party, but tonight she was making her favourite curry and she wasn't planning on sharing it with anyone.

On the way home from work, she stopped off at the local supermarket and bought all the necessary ingredients. And after a long, warm soak in scented bath oils, she padded into her kitchen, drew the red gingham curtains closed and slipped her favourite Spanish guitar CD into the player.

In the four years she'd worked for Tropicana Films, she'd always made a deliberate effort to separate her work and her leisure. At the end of the working day, she relished time for herself to clear her thoughts. Now it was especially important to forget about her new boss and the persistent, niggling worry that he might have recognised her as the figure flaunting herself in Henry's doorway.

What if Henry had said something to Mitch?

Shaking her head furiously, she tried to push aside such invasive thoughts and turned up the volume on the CD player. The fluid sounds rippled around her and she began to feel better than she had in days.

Three days.

She hummed softly under her breath as she diced lamb, and chopped onions and garlic. And within twenty minutes the small kitchen was redolent with the rich fragrance of lamb simmering in curry leaves, fresh coriander, crushed cummin and chilli.

Totally absorbed in her task, she was stirring in the final ingredient, coconut milk, when a knock on her door startled her. Quickly, she lowered the heat and snatched up a towel to wipe her hands as she headed for the door.

The last person she expected to find on her doorstep was Mitch Wentworth. Grace's heart plummeted.

'Wow, something smells wonderful.' He sniffed the air appreciatively.

'Er, hello, Mr Wentworth,' she murmured, only just resisting the temptation to slam the door in his face. At least she was fully clothed this time. Not that her favourite old tracksuit was exactly suitable attire for greeting the boss. Especially when he was still in the elegantly tailored business suit he wore to the office. Her hand strayed to her hair which, aided by the soak in the bath and the warmth of the kitchen, had loosened and begun to fall in wispy strands around her face. She rubbed one bare foot against the other. 'What can I do for you?'

'Do I smell roghan josh curry?' Mitch asked.

Her eyes widened. 'Madras, actually,' she answered warily. Surely he wasn't looking for a meal?

'Ah, yes. I should have noticed.' Mitch smiled and Grace took a step back. She needed to put some distance between herself and that smile. 'There is faint aroma of coconut,' he agreed. 'Roghan josh has yoghurt, doesn't it?'

'You—you like curries?' Why did she ask? Every man she'd ever met liked curries. But rarely were they so familiar with the details of the ingredients. 'This one needs to simmer for a good while yet,' she hastened to add, in case he had any bright ideas about inviting himself for dinner.

'There's no need to look so nervous, Grace. I won't be invading your privacy for very long,' Mitch reassured her as if he'd been reading her mind. 'And I'm sure Henry Aspinall would have something to say if I ate his share of dinner.'

'Hen—Henry?' Grace stammered. *What exactly did he know about Henry?*

'He's been chasing me to look at his graphic designs and when I first met him he mentioned you and he were…good friends.'

'Oh.' Grace gulped. Nervously, she waited to see if Mitch was going to expand on this information. When he didn't, she added, 'So why have you come here?'

'Do you mind if I come in for just a moment? There are a few things I need to discuss with you and I'd like to clear them up tonight.'

Mitch expected her hesitation, but he also knew Grace would invite him in. She had seen that he was holding the folder with her report and curiosity sparked from her green eyes. Valiantly ignoring his hunger pangs, he followed her into the small sitting room, rich with the fragrant, spicy smells that drifted from her kitchen.

He couldn't help noticing that it was a lovely room— not extravagantly decorated, but comfortable and welcoming. And the raw, emotive passion of the guitar music in the background was a surprise. Another layer to the Grace Robbins enigma.

Mitch's gaze roved slowly around the cosy setting. The lighting was low, creating a soothing mood. And the warm, natural earth colours of the terracotta tiled floor and the two large Aboriginal paintings dominating the main wall gave a sense of mellowness. In the opposite corner, beneath a black and white movie poster of Bogey and Bacall, a fat earthenware pot held a sheaf of dried grasses. Beside it sat an overly plump floor cushion covered with a stone-and claret-coloured design.

He'd rarely settled in one spot long enough to establish his own home, but when he did make purchases these same earthy tones, sunburnt ochres and browns were the colours that always attracted him.

The chocolate brown sofa was deep and soft and Mitch sank into it gratefully. Grace sat opposite him on a woven cane chair and clutched at a sienna and black striped cushion as if her life depended on it. Nevertheless, he didn't miss the way she curled into the deep chair with catlike elegance.

'You decorated this place yourself?' he asked.

'Yes. I thought the *New Tomorrow* project would take long enough to warrant moving all my gear from Sydney.'

Mitch nodded. 'It's very attractive. I'm looking forward to finding a home base for myself.' His glance drifted to the fish tank on a stand behind her chair. Two goldfish and a black fish. 'I have a sister-in-law who is a feng shui expert. She claims that aquariums are very helpful for creating…' he paused, searching for the right word, but gave up with a smiling shrug '…a happy environment.'

Grace's mouth twitched as she gestured to the fish. 'I've read that. These guys are the Marx Brothers.'

'Let me guess. The black one is Groucho.'

'Of course.' She laughed. Then she looked startled as if she hadn't meant to let down her guard. 'Um—what did you want to speak about?'

She was edgy—probably in a hurry to get rid of him before Aspinall turned up. Mitch suppressed a sigh as he pictured the other man wolfing down her delicious meal. He avoided thinking of any other delights in store for Henry Aspinall by flipping her report onto his knee and tapping his finger against the cover. 'This is good, Grace. Very good. I have to say I'm very impressed by how quickly you've made yourself familiar with the North Queensland territory.'

Her eyes lit up with pleasure. Mitch found their sudden sparkle arresting.

'It's very interesting country,' Grace replied, unconsciously crossing one long, towelling-clad leg over the other. 'As I said in my report, I think there are many location options on our back doorstep.'

Mitch had never noticed before just how sexy faded blue terry towelling could be. He dragged his gaze away. Her body shouldn't, couldn't be a factor here. Praising her business skills was the way to win over Grace Robbins. 'Your report is very persuasive. That's why I'm here tonight. I'd like to start investigating some of these outback locations straight away.'

'Immediately?'

'Tomorrow morning.'

She nodded thoughtfully and Mitch could sense her thoughts whirling behind those wide green eyes as she calculated what needed to be done. 'You'd definitely check out Undara?' she queried.

He referred to his scribbled notes. 'The ancient lava tubes? Yes. They sound fantastic for the underground scenes. And I want to look at some of the old deserted mining towns, too.'

'Like Ravenswood or the Mount Surprise district?'

'They're the ones.' Mitch nodded.

'You'd hire a four-wheel drive?'

Mitch could tell that she was catching onto his enthusiasm. The cushion she'd been clutching earlier slipped unheeded to the floor.

'I think that would be best. Then I could mosey on and explore more of the outback. I want to take a good look at the Gulf country. There's so much great wilderness terrain out there.'

'And with its own peculiar kind of beauty,' Grace supplied. She leaned forward, an excited pink tinting her cheeks. 'I'm sure you'll find just what you're looking for in the Gulf.'

For the briefest moment, Mitch had the eerie feeling that there was something deeply prophetic about her words—as if he would actually find something much more meaningful than a location for his film. He blinked and shook his head. Grace might be clever, but she could not see into the future. Working overtime on top of jet lag could produce the weirdest sensations.

He smiled at her. 'You understand what I'm looking for, don't you?'

'I—I think so.' Perhaps he was staring too intently. Her cheeks grew pinker and she looked away for a moment.

'This industry is a dog-eat-dog world. And filming at a great location will give my movie the kind of competitive edge I need.'

She seemed to recover, giving a little shake, and as she spoke she met him once more with a level gaze. 'As I understand it, you're hoping to create a kind post-World War III scenario—a world where the people who are left will start all over again. The old world is lost or contaminated except for this small section of land and it is pure and unpolluted. So you want something isolated—pristine, untouched.'

Mitch jumped to his feet. 'That's exactly what I'm looking for. It's great that you understand. And that's why you'll be coming with me.'

The look of horror that swept across her features shocked him. He hadn't expected opposition from someone so deeply involved with the film.

'You'll help me check out the locations, of course.'

'Oh, no. I can't. I—I can't possibly,' she stammered.

'Why not?' He'd set his mind on having her with him. Her knowledge, the research she'd already undertaken, was invaluable.

'I have so much to do.' Her hands were twisting ner-

vously in her lap. She looked so frightened, Mitch wanted
to grab her by the shoulders and shake some sense into her.
What kind of a man did she think he was?

'I'm the boss, Grace. I know exactly what you have to
do. And I know you can spare the time for this trip.'

What had he done wrong to upset her so badly? How
could she be so keen one minute and then suddenly back
off as if he'd turned into a ghoulish monster? Mitch paced
the length of her fashionable hand-woven rug. Caught up
with the positive tone of her report, he had come tonight
with the expectation that Grace would see it as her professional duty to accompany him—no matter what her personal hang-ups were. And now he was prepared to be as
stubborn as was necessary.

He wasn't leaving until she said *yes*.

# CHAPTER FOUR

'GRACE, I'm offering you a chance to get out of the office—to get away in the outback and to really explore this project with me. How could you refuse?'

'By saying no!' she snapped, and leapt to her feet. She was incensed by Mitch's arrogant assumption that she'd give her eye-teeth to slip away with him. 'I realise that's probably a new experience for you, Mr Wentworth.'

He shot her a startled glance, before throwing his head back and releasing a quiet chuckle. 'Of course I've had my share of rejections, Ms Robbins.'

Mitch eyed her shrewdly while he paced her floor and Grace felt like a witness in the dock about to be cross-examined. There was a long, awkward silence before he spoke again. 'Would we be talking about relationships here? The man-woman kind? Or are we talking about business and the world at large?'

She didn't answer, but when he retaliated by crossing the short strip of matting towards her Grace held her breath, desperately willing her heart to stay calm and wishing that she could think of a smart retort that would stop him in his tracks. In spite of all the warnings her mind issued, her body started overreacting whenever this man got close. He must know the effect he had on women. He should be considerate and keep his distance.

'Which Grace Robbins is rejecting my request?' Mitch drawled softly, while he shook her report in her face. 'The Grace who wrote this report wouldn't hesitate to help check out these locations.'

Suddenly she was very unsure of her ground.

'Is there something deeper going down here?' Mitch frowned and rubbed his chin thoughtfully. 'Perhaps I was wrong to throw that magazine with your artwork in the bin and assume we could start afresh? Do you dislike me so much that you can't bear to make this journey in my company?'

She shook her head, trying to convince herself that her protests were well-founded, but for the life of her Grace couldn't articulate her objections. Surely she had good, solid, professional reasons to offer him beyond the pitiful fact that he was so sexy that her clear thinking, precise mind turned to candy floss when he was around? And now he expected her to go away with him!

Just the two of them!

Until now she had always been prepared to cooperate wholeheartedly with her employer. But her previous boss, George Hervey, had been a thoughtful and considerate, elderly gentleman. Working for him, she had always felt safe and sure of her role.

Now, trying to come up with a plausible explanation for her refusal, she couldn't get her head past Mitch's suggestion that her objections were more to do with how she felt about him than how she felt about her work.

Mitch was still spearing her with his dark gaze. 'Would it make a difference if I promised Henry Aspinall not to lay a finger on you for the duration of the journey?' he asked.

'Henry?' Her cheeks flamed. Why did he keep mentioning Henry? 'Henry has nothing to do with this. He's mistaken if he thinks we're still…friends.'

'Indeed?' He considered her response for another uncomfortably long moment. 'You look terrified. What is there to be afraid of?'

Mitch stepped forward and, with an assurance she was sure came from years of experience, reached out his hand to rest it lightly at the nape of her neck. Her skin grew hot beneath his touch and she fully intended to pull away. But, with the same ease that a bright flower attracts a giddy butterfly, he slowly drew her towards him and her good intentions melted. Her lips hovered just below his. 'Is this what you're frightened of, Grace?'

Her heart fluttered frantically.

There was no doubt he intended to kiss her.

And Grace also sensed at that moment, that if she cried out, or tried to beat Mitch Wentworth off with her fists, he would certainly let her go. She might have asked him to stop if she hadn't been having such difficulty with her breathing, but instead she allowed him to close that last short gap.

As Mitch's warm mouth settled over hers, a tiny sob escaped her and she felt him pull away slightly.

But she was already under his spell.

Her eyes were already closed and her face was tilted at a shamefully helpful angle. And, after that one brief touch of his lips, she was mentally begging him to taste her, to explore her mouth with his own. And when he did Grace sank against him as if she needed his strength.

There was nothing arrogant or pigheaded about the way Mitch's hands tenderly cradled her face, or the way his mouth lazily investigated hers. It was a journey of discovery beyond her wildest dreams. Wherever he touched her, her skin seemed to flare with delicious sensitivity. The way his mouth moved, slowly and seductively against hers, felt so-o-o good. Utterly spellbound, Grace's lips opened, pleading for more. Mitch's kiss deepened and, as if they had a mind of their own, her arms rose shyly to link themselves around his neck.

There was nothing threatening about being in his embrace. Never before had she felt so womanly, so desirable, so eager for a man to explore *more* than her lips. When Mitch finally broke away, it took all her strength of will not to moan in soft protest.

He looked down at her, his gaze smoky with emotion. 'Another question answered,' he murmured softly.

And the spell was broken.

Shocked, Grace staggered backwards, her hand at her mouth as if she couldn't quite believe she'd allowed such a thing to happen.

'What do you think you're doing? You can't just get your way by trying to seduce me,' she cried, her voice shrill with self-recrimination.

'Of course not,' Mitch responded quickly. 'I wasn't using a kiss as a persuasive device. It was just—how shall I put it? An experiment. I needed to discover something.'

Incensed, Grace grabbed a sofa cushion and hurled it at him. 'How dare you? How *could* you experiment with me?'

Mitch caught the cushion neatly and stood holding it in both hands. Hands which only minutes earlier had been caressing her. 'I don't know, Grace,' he replied, a tiny smile playing at the corners of his mouth. 'Can you explain how we seem to be such a great team when it comes to kissing?'

Of course she couldn't! It was the stupidest thing she'd ever done. Well, almost, she corrected as her memory replayed two other occasions this week when she'd made a first-class fool of herself in front of this man.

'Don't think a little kiss will make me want to go off travelling in the outback alone with you,' she hissed.

'What if I promise never to kiss you again?'

'Oh?' Grace gasped. *Never?* She hoped her reply held no echo of the ridiculous wave of regret that flooded right through her.

'Boy scout's honour,' Mitch replied, tossing her a grin and a two fingered salute. Then he shot her a cheeky sideways glance and added, 'Of course, I'd be prepared to build in an escape clause.'

'Escape?' she echoed faintly.

'I'll only kiss you if you want me to. The next time I take you in my arms will be when you ask me to, Ms Robbins.'

That brought her to her senses. 'In your dreams, Wentworth.'

'I'm afraid I can't promise what might happen in them.'

Grace glared at him as she folded her arms across her chest and took several deep, fortifying breaths. The impact of that kiss was still reverberating through her body. Her heartbeats weren't just racing, they were stampeding. Anybody would think she'd never been kissed before. She suppressed the recognition that she had never been kissed like *that* before. Roger the Rat had been nowhere near as good.

To think she'd joked the other day about playing with the big boys. Clearly, Mitch's kisses were in a league of their own.

His businesslike tone cut through her wayward thoughts. 'I really do need you to make this trip with me. You understand exactly what I want. You've already done all the groundwork. No one else will be nearly as useful. Give me some credit. I swear I'm not a boss who preys on his female staff. I want us to work together as a great business team.'

*Forget about the kiss,* she chided. *He means it. It's not going to happen again. Concentrate on the job.* 'How many days would we be away?' she asked softly.

Mitch beamed at her. 'I knew you wouldn't let me down.' He glanced again at the notes he'd made on the end of her report. 'Five days should just about do the trick.'

She nodded weakly.

His answering nod of acceptance, as if he knew all along that she would capitulate, annoyed Grace, but she forced her mind to stay focused on practical business details. 'Do we need to make any bookings?'

'I'll book for tomorrow night at Undara,' he replied. 'After that I'd like to be as flexible as possible. We'll take my mobile phone and book ahead as we go.' Mitch's eyebrows rose and he jerked his head in the direction of her kitchen. 'That curry of yours should be just about ready by now, shouldn't it?'

'Don't push your luck, Mr Wentworth,' Grace warned, pointing to her door. 'If I have to spend the next five days with my boss, I need a little solitude tonight.' More than anything else, she needed to think about how on earth she'd ever allowed that kiss to happen.

Her very worst fears about Mitch had already proved well-founded. He was the kind of man who could charm a nun away from her prayers. And now she was going to be travelling alone with him! Grace believed he'd keep his promise about not kissing her again, but she needed to develop strategies to ensure her body didn't come up with any silly ideas of its own.

Mitch didn't try to hide his disappointment that he wouldn't taste her curry, but to her relief he had just enough manners not to push the matter. 'I'll have the vehicle ready for nine o'clock in the morning,' he said as he went through her doorway. 'I'll pick you up from here.'

Punctuality was not her boss's strongest feature, Grace decided next morning when he eventually pulled up outside her flat a good thirty minutes late. He was driving a large, solid-looking off-road vehicle with a tray back.

She had expected something more flashy and sporty—

perhaps a shiny black and gold, city-style, four-wheel drive. This was a regular bush vehicle.

When Mitch swung the driver's door open and jumped down, flashing her a boyish grin, she was surprised by the way her own spirits lifted. She was hardly feeling her best after a long night tossing restlessly in her bed, worrying about spending five days rattling around the North Queensland outback side by side with her employer.

But this morning, dressed in jeans and an army-green bush shirt, he was looking so genuinely excited, like a boy allowed off on his very first Huckleberry Finn adventure, that her fears subsided somewhat. His enthusiasm, as he patted the truck's sturdy bonnet, was almost infectious. Not that she was prepared to let him see a chink in her armour. She nodded an unsmiling greeting.

Mitch wasn't to be put off. 'I've made sure I got a vehicle fitted out with absolutely everything we could possibly need. Spare water tanks, special tow ropes and winches in case we get bogged. Tarps and cooking gear if we decide to rough it. That's why I'm a bit late—making sure we had all those extras.'

'Did you get G.P.S.?'

'A global positioning system?' Mitch frowned, looking slightly put out. 'What do you know about that sort of thing?'

'Oh…' she shrugged '…I've read about it. It seems like a brilliant system for making sure you don't get lost. The army use it a lot.'

'I doubt we'll need gear that sophisticated to help us navigate. We've got maps and a mobile phone and a good sturdy vehicle—and neither of us is a fool. We're not going to get lost.'

'I guess not,' she agreed, but she pulled a face that allowed just a hint of doubt to linger in the air as she lifted her carefully packed kit bag and heaved it onto one shoulder.

'Here, let me take that,' he offered.

Finding it rather a strain to remain ungracious in the face of his helpfulness, Grace allowed him to take her pack. As she did so, he dipped his face close to hers and his dark eyes danced as they studied her. 'Aha! I think I detect a faint smile,' he teased.

'A slip of the lip,' muttered Grace.

Mitch sighed as he hefted her bag into the back of the truck. 'So that's the way it's going to be, is it, Ms Robbins?' His glance slid to her jeans. 'Five days of venom in denim.'

His words found their mark and Grace's cheeks burned. Perhaps she was behaving unprofessionally—more like an immature kid.

'Sorry,' she said, shooting him a fair attempt at a smile. 'I'm a bit tired.'

'Then you should just sit back and relax and let me take care of the driving. Did you want to bring any of your favourite CDs to help while away the miles?'

She stared back at him, surprised. 'That's a great idea! I won't be long.' About to dash into her flat, she paused. 'Do you have any preferences?'

Mitch leant his long frame against the truck's door and sent her a slow, conspiratorial smile. 'I think there's a very good chance we have similar tastes, Grace. I'm prepared to go along with whatever you choose.'

As she collected a pile of CDs, she sensed her mouth softening into the beginnings of a genuine smile.

Grace wasn't sure who was more surprised, she or Mitch, when they covered the six-hour journey up the narrow road to Undara without any sparring or tense silences. They only saw a few vehicles during the journey. They listened to her music, chatted about *New Tomorrow,* about people they knew in the film industry, or sat in comfortable silence as the countryside flashed past them in streaks of brown and grey-green against a bright blue sky. There were even moments when she actually laughed out loud at stories he told about colourful Hollywood personalities.

But whenever she started to relax Grace quickly reminded herself to be wary of her boss. He could pour on the charm when it suited him, but she knew from bitter experience that she must never lower her resistance.

From time to time Mitch stopped the truck to look at a point of interest. A flock of emus caught his attention, and he slowed to take a closer look.

'I'll bring them in near us,' he told her.

Grace eyed him dubiously. 'So what exactly are you going to do? Warble their mating call?'

He darted a withering glance in her direction. 'Just watch this, city girl.' Winding down his window, he held out his wide-brimmed hat and waved it at the emus. The birds stopped abruptly, staring at the movement. As Mitch continued waving, one of the scraggy, long-legged birds slowly stepped forward, a beady eye fixed on the hat. Then the others followed cautiously, until several dark-feathered adults and three stripy chicks were all gathered at the edge of the highway, staring fiercely at Mitch and his hat.

'That's a cool trick,' breathed Grace. 'Where'd you learn it?'

'Oh, I knocked about in the bush quite a bit when I was younger. I'm not a complete city slicker. Look!' He pointed as one of the adults herded up the chicks. 'You don't often see the mother emu with her babies.'

Grace cleared her throat. 'Actually, city boy, it's the male emu that incubates the eggs and looks after the chicks.'

'Poor bloke,' Mitch muttered under his breath as he accelerated back onto the highway. He shot Grace a baleful glance. 'And where did you learn that?'

'Oh, I read a lot…' she answered airily.

They travelled on, companionably silent, as the bush flashed past them—the rough black trunks of ironbarks, the silvery smooth limbs of woollybutts and the deeper red of bloodwoods.

Later in the day, more animals emerged. A butcher-bird startled Grace when it took off suddenly from the side of the road with a long, thin snake in its beak. In the shadowy verges, kangaroos and wallabies slowly edged out for an afternoon graze. It was late in the day by the time they rattled down the final stretch of dirt road to reach Undara.

'You've organised our accommodation, haven't you?' she asked warily.

'Sure have,' Mitch assured her. 'We're also booked in for a meal tonight and our underground tour in the morning. I'll just head into the office there and pick up our keys.'

Grace watched as he bounded up the three steps and crossed the timber veranda to the reception area. Somehow, despite his city lifestyle, Grace had to admit that Mitch had avoided the urban cowboy image. He really looked as at home in faded blue jeans and scuffed riding boots in the bush as he did in his expensive Italian suits and hand-stitched, shining shoes in the city.

She had the uncomfortable feeling that Mitch was the kind of guy who would look good in any setting—in any clothes. Or without clothes, came the errant thought. She dismissed it quickly.

As he headed back to the truck, he was frowning. He flipped open the door and swung his long frame into the driver's seat. 'Minor hitch,' he mumbled.

Grace's heart jumped a beat or two. 'How's that?' she whispered.

'I don't know how it happened, but there's been a mis-understanding about our accommodation.'

'A misunderstanding? Didn't you know the accommodation here is converted railway carriages?'

'Yeah. That's not the problem.' His dark eyes rested on her and his mouth twisted into a lopsided grin. 'Actually, there's no problem really. At least, there won't be if you don't throw a tantrum.'

Alarm sent tiny shivers darting through Grace's innards. 'Tantrum?' she squeaked and then she struggled to gain more composure. 'I haven't thrown a tantrum since I was two years old. For heaven's sake, what are you rambling on about?'

He twisted the key in the ignition and, as the engine chugged back to life, he told her. 'A couple of busloads of tourists have filled the place up and there's only one spot left for us. Honestly, I don't know how they got the idea we were a couple.'

Grace shot him a suspicious glare. 'You—you mean we have to share a…'

'A room,' Mitch supplied.

'Twin share?'

''Fraid not. Double.'

'We can't!' Grace yelled back. She ran nervous hands through her hair. The comfortable safety shield she'd been building all day had suddenly developed huge gaping cracks. 'This is ridiculous!' she shouted.

'We're not in the city now, Grace. In the bush you take what's offered.' Mitch nudged the truck towards the distant row of brown-painted railway carriages lined up in the shade of gum trees. 'In case you didn't know, beds are for sleeping, not just for sex. We can build a little barricade with pillows.'

Grace clamped her teeth closed as a screech of frustration threatened.

Mitch shot her a sideways glance. 'I didn't think you'd take this news too calmly. Look, it's a long drive back to anywhere else and we'd only have to come back out here again in the morning,' he commented. 'You get all kinds of hazards in remote areas, but I'm game if you are.'

'Of course you are!' she cried.

Mitch stopped in their allotted parking bay, outlined by rough bush timber, cut off the engine and turned to her. 'What's that supposed to mean?'

'It's no skin off your nose to spend one more night in bed with a woman you hardly know. It—it's your—*hobby*!' She flung her hands upwards to emphasise her words.

Mitch grabbed the hand nearest him and held it in a vice-like grip. 'If we're talking about hobbies, Ms Robbins, perhaps I should remind you that I've been an eyewitness to an interesting hobby of yours. It's not every girl who has a penchant for greeting men at the front door in her underwear.'

*Oh, no!* Grace's mouth hung open as she stared at Mitch in speechless horror. *All this time he'd known!*

For several long seconds, Mitch eyed her sternly and his grip on her hand tightened. 'So now you can stop behaving like a puritan and be adult about this. I've already seen what you have on offer. And, for Pete's sake, I've already promised I won't touch you.' He dropped her hand and swung his door open. 'If you'd like to be first in the shower, it's at the end of the carriage and you'd better get moving.'

With stiff, robotic movements, Grace climbed out of the truck, while her mind recoiled from the onslaught of Mitch's speech. She wasn't sure what had offended her more—his revelations about the embarrassing episode in Henry's flat, the claim that she was behaving like a silly little girl, or the implication that he wasn't remotely interested in her as a woman.

*Get a grip, girl!* she chided herself as she followed him into the carriage. *One minute you're terrified this man might touch you, the next you're upset because he promises not to.*

She'd been making Mount Everest out of a molehill. The very fact that he hadn't mentioned the incident at Henry's flat until now proved that her boss was no more interested in her personal life than she was in his.

It was important to remember that, just because she couldn't help thinking about his kiss and the delightful way he'd touched and held her as if she were a very special prize, there was no chance Mitch Wentworth actually considered her as anything other than his efficient employee. And that was, after all, what she wanted.

Maybe his kiss had scored right off the Richter scale, but she would have to put it out of her mind. He had probably forgotten about it before he'd left her flat. He'd been more interested in her curry than her kiss.

Nevertheless, the relaxed camaraderie they'd enjoyed during the day was rather more strained at dinner. The threat of the night ahead loomed over Grace and as she sat opposite Mitch, she felt ridiculously nervous.

Undara Lodge's dining area was a wide timber deck protected from the elements by huge canvas awnings, and all around them relaxed and happy tourists laughed and chatted in a mixture of languages. Their mood contrasted sharply with Grace's. These were people on holiday, keen for adventure in the Australian outback and having a good time.

She toyed with her chicken marinated in wine, wattle seeds and mountain pepper and Mitch tucked into Georgetown sausages while he outlined the key factors they needed to focus on when they toured the lava tubes in the morning.

But Grace knew he was laughing at her embarrassment and inner turmoil.

On the surface he appeared cool and businesslike as he flipped a small notebook out of his shirt pocket and made notes of pertinent questions they needed to ask if they wanted to use this site as a film location. But she could tell that he was laughing inside. The playful spark in his eyes betrayed him.

'I presume that amongst all this reading you do, you've boned up on the geological formation of these tubes?' he asked.

Grace patted her lips with her serviette and replied with as much dignity as she could muster. 'As a matter of fact, yes, I have.'

'Can you give it to me in language a simple movie man can understand?'

She took a sip from her wineglass and favoured him with what she hoped was a look icy enough to freeze the smile right off his face. 'A hundred and ninety thousand years ago, volcanoes erupted in this area and huge rivers of lava spilled everywhere, mainly following the old water courses. As they flowed, the lava on the outside cooled at a faster rate and it began to harden, but the very hot lava at the core kept flowing, pushing a hollow tunnel inside. The tubes here are the best preserved and most impressive in the world.'

'Thank you, Grace.' A small muscle near the corner of his mouth twitched as he poured some more wine into their glasses.

Grace stared at her plate in silent rage. She was more sure than ever that, while Mitch appeared to be polite and detached, he was playing with her, in much the same way a cat toyed with a mouse.

How on earth had she got to this point? She hadn't

wanted to share office space with this arrogant man who'd blasted his way into the company, and now she was sharing—*his bed!*

By the time Mitch had finished his first course, she was a dithering mess. 'I'm not very hungry,' she said as she placed her knife and fork very carefully to one side of the half-eaten meal on her plate. 'I won't worry about dessert or coffee. But please, you stay and have as much as you like.'

Mitch stood politely as she left the table. 'Make sure you're tucked in tight and sound asleep before I get back,' he said softly, while his eyes danced with undisguised amusement.

Grace's shoulders stiffened. 'You're being utterly detestable,' she sneered over her shoulder as she sailed off the deck.

Storming down the short bush path to their carriage, she charged inside and banged the door. She leaned against it, shaking. He was hateful! How could poor George Hervey possibly enjoy his enforced retirement when he knew this bully boy was wrecking their happy little company? He might have money and ideas, but Mitch Wentworth's people skills left a lot to be desired!

Still raging, she changed into her pyjamas. Thank goodness she had a sensible cotton pair with a high neck, long sleeves and long legs. It was a pity they were hot pink and dotted with little white hearts, but at least they left no part of her exposed. She tucked the top into the trousers and drew the drawstring tightly into her waist before securing it with a double knot.

Then she removed her make-up and cleaned her teeth. About to leave the bathroom, Grace paused, and, avoiding the message her reflection revealed about how distraught and anxious she looked, she inspected her teeth in the mirror, and cleaned them again. And she dabbed some perfume behind her ears. Then she stared at her reflection, horrified. Why on earth did she want to smell nice?

Shaking with confusion, she carefully drew back the bedspread and climbed between the sheets. Then, rolling onto her side, she turned out the bedside lamp. In the dark, she lay ramrod-stiff with the sheet tucked high beneath her chin and waited for the sound of Mitch's returning footsteps...

But, no matter how hard she tried, Grace couldn't stop her wretched mind from imagining the night ahead. What was it going to be like, lying side by side with Mitch? Would he stick to his half of the bed? Would he roll onto his back and fling one arm out so that he touched her? And what would she do then? Might they wake in the morning to find themselves wrapped in each other's arms?

As she lay in the dark room, listening to the creak of the overhead fan, her tortuous imagination played out dozens of possible and impossible scenarios until she wanted to scream with the stress of it all. How could this same brain that served her so methodically and well when it came to assimilating information and absorbing facts turn itself inside out when she contemplated Mitch Wentworth?

Everything about him—his good looks, his powerful presence, his annoying self-confidence—placed her on the alert. Mitch was so much like Roger. Such men ate young women for breakfast before heading off to build their empires.

Were there no decent men in this world? Roger had broken her heart. Henry had enraged her. And Mitch?

*Mitch doesn't factor in this equation,* she reminded herself. *He's a boss, not a boyfriend.*

But any tensions Grace experienced when she first went to bed were magnified a hundred times over during the next hour or so. Rather than hearing footsteps returning to the cabins, the only sounds that drifted on the still night air were laughter and happy voices coming from the diners on the deck. Out in the bush, everything else was so very quiet that these sounds seemed even louder than normal. And, as the weary night wore on, the cheery voices grew merrier— probably as people drank more, she guessed. She could tell by the sudden guffaws of laughter that jokes were being shared and glasses were being clinked together in endless toasts.

Mitch had no doubt forgotten all about her and was joining in the fun. And, of course, the harder she tried to get to sleep, the wider awake she became!

When she heard the strains of 'Waltzing Matilda' sung in a mixture of German, Danish and English accents, Grace snatched up a second pillow and tried to block out the gaiety. She hoped every single one of those people had a huge hangover in the morning.

Eventually, after an interminable wait, the voices separated and she heard people moving to their carriages. At long last her own door was pushed open. Grace lay rigid with tension as she listened to Mitch stumbling around in the dark. She heard one thump then another as his boots hit the floor—the scrape of his zip and the slide of denim as he stripped off his jeans. Any minute now, she would feel the mattress give as he lowered his long frame onto it...

# CHAPTER FIVE

GRACE held her breath.

There was a little more quiet scuffling and bumping, and then silence.

And more silence.

Alert as a time bomb about to explode, she lay in the bed desperately trying to make sense of this lack of sound. Where on earth had Mitch gone now? A sickening thought struck her. Had he crept out to visit someone else's bed? Not knowing was more than she could bear. She snapped on the bedside light.

'What's going on?' From the floor on the far side of the room, Mitch sat up, blinking.

She could only see him from the waist up, and as far as she could tell he wasn't wearing anything. He was looking tousled and tired, and in the soft lamplight she found herself staring at the tumble of hair in his eyes, the late-night shadow on his jaw, the breadth of his shoulders. The visible half of his body was as sleek and beautifully muscled as a sculpture by Michelangelo.

'I—I didn't know where you were,' she stammered. 'What are you doing on the floor?'

'Trying to sleep,' he muttered.

'But—but why down there?'

He rubbed his eyes sleepily, then blinked again before staring back at her. She sank against the pillows as the slow-burning pressure of his gaze set her heart scampering into a crazy, dancing rhythm. This was how he'd looked at her last night—just before he'd kissed her.

Then he grinned through the gloom. 'It's okay, Grace. I spoke to the management and explained about our...our little problem. They were great. They lent me a swag, so I'm fine. I'll kip down here tonight.'

As he settled back onto the floor, Grace flicked off the light and hot anger seethed through her entire body. It was so ridiculous! Mitch was handling this awkward situation like a gentleman and she should be grateful. Of course she was grateful!

*Why wasn't she grateful?*

She flung herself restlessly across the bed, trying to find a comfortable position, and his disembodied voice reached her through the darkness.

'It was a pity you were so tired; you missed a great party.'

Somehow she managed to turn a scream of fury into a mumbled, 'G'night.'

One last time, his voice, deep and rich as chocolate liqueur, came through the night. 'Pink looks okay on you, but not as sexy as black lace.'

After that Grace spent a long, empty night tossing and turning while she listened to Mitch's regular, relaxed breathing.

The Undara lava tubes blew Mitch away. He had expected the underground formations to be interesting, and he'd hoped they would be grand, but he'd never expected them to be quite so spectacular.

'Blow me if this isn't just too good to be true,' he whispered to Grace as they followed the trail of tourists along the wooden walkway in the first enormous lava tunnel. High above them, like the richly decorated ceiling of a towering cathedral, arched glorious patterns. The intricate red, pink, ochre and cream designs, which, their guide explained, had formed when iron and calcium leached through the basalt, would look superb through a camera lens. 'Couldn't be better for what we want!' he enthused. 'The scenes dealing with underground survivors are so vital to the movie. This is magnificent!' He patted Grace's shoulder. 'And *you're* magnificent.'

She jumped at his touch and turned startled green eyes his way. 'I beg your pardon?'

'You showed a masterstroke of pure genius when you suggested checking out these tubes.'

Grace blinked at his praise. 'I realised they must be pretty sensational when I read that you could fit two trains on railway tracks in here and there'd still be room for another level on top of that.'

'We could never create anything quite so awe-inspiring with computer graphics, or by trying to build a set in a studio.' Mitch realised his hand was still resting on her shoulder. She was wearing some kind of halter-neck cotton top and her shoulder was bare. Beneath his fingers, Grace's skin was silky and soft and he was surprised by his urge to give her shoulder an enthusiastic squeeze.

Not a wise move, Wentworth, he reflected with a laconic shrug. Best to change his line of thinking before he did something he regretted.

But, as they continued into a narrower section of the stone tunnel, the surroundings became less absorbing and Mitch became much more conscious of Grace's perfume filling the enclosed space. The scent she wore was very fresh and flowery, without being too sweet. And every so often, he caught traces of the fragrance of her hair. There was nothing artificial about its smell, and it reminded him of a fresh autumn morning, gentle sunlight and clean, tangy lemons.

'What are you doing?' Grace's sharp words in his ear

cut into his wandering thoughts. What *was* he doing? How had his arm crept back around her shoulders? He dropped it abruptly.

'Got carried away with the excitement of all this natural splendour,' he responded, in what he hoped was a deceptively casual reply. He diverted his attention to the primeval rock formations around them, rather than the neat curve and slope of her shoulders and the straight, perfect symmetry of her collarbones—natural splendours, way out of his territory. 'Don't the psychologists tell us the cave represents the womb?' he elaborated. 'It must be why I'm feeling kind of…primitive.'

Grace opened her mouth as if to comment, but must have thought better of it.

'What about you?' he joked. 'Any primitive urges?'

'I—I feel perfectly normal,' she said, defying her words by nervously wiping her hands on her linen shorts.

Mitch considered the way she walked a little faster, putting more distance between them. This puzzling woman was getting under his skin. There was so much that he liked about her and yet, around him, she was permanently uptight—always on tenterhooks, as if she suspected he would pounce on her and have his wicked way with her at any moment.

Anyone would think she'd lived her life locked away in a tower.

But that couldn't be the case. He'd seen her looking more sexy and alluring in fetching black lingerie than any siren of the silver screen. And the other night, when he'd kissed her—why, her enjoyment had been breathtakingly unrestrained. He'd been absolutely stunned by the eagerness of her sweet, receptive mouth and the yearning he'd sensed in her soft, submissive body—as if she'd come to life in his arms.

It was a fanciful notion, but, for a moment, she'd made him feel like the prince who kissed Sleeping Beauty, waking her from one hundred years' sleep.

How he'd walked out of that flat without throwing her onto the sofa and taking her there and then was nothing short of miraculous. Perhaps Grace had every right to be nervous of him.

It was mid-afternoon before they finished their interviews with the management at Undara. They were delighted to discover that obtaining the official permits for filming would not be a problem, as long as Tropicana contracted to meet certain environmental considerations.

Once they left, Mitch was determined to head further north-west, to explore what he called the real Gulf country. 'I'm not sure of exactly what I want, but I'm looking for something stark. I'll know it when I see it,' he told Grace.

And she had to be content with that.

In a way she was rather grateful to be able to sit back and let the miles drift by as Mitch drove through the late afternoon. They didn't bother much with conversation. She'd spent the last two nights tossing sleeplessly and now she was weary. And, with Gershwin's 'Rhapsody in Blue' playing softly while the truck sped along the straight, monotonous stretch of road towards Georgetown, she felt herself nodding off.

Luckily, Mitch seemed caught up in his own thoughts as he stared ahead at the single-lane bitumen road. It looked like a thin, red-stained ribbon stretching across the wide savannah. She made a pillow by folding her leather jacket and propping it up against the window. Curling up her legs as best she could, she rested her head against it. Before too long, she drifted off to sleep...

\*    \*    \*

Her forehead banging hard against the window woke her.

It was dark. Grace struggled into consciousness, surprised to discover that their truck was swaying, banging and thumping its way through the dark across very rough and rocky terrain. Feeling stiff and a little groggy from sleep, she struggled to sit straight. Her neck was cricked and sore from the way she'd slept.

'Where are we? Where's the road?' she mumbled as she tried to make sense of the brief glimpses of wild landscape shown up by the jumping headlights.

'Good evening,' Mitch grinned. 'You're awake.'

She was about to ask the time, but the clock on the dashboard in front of her told her that it was almost eight o'clock. 'Good heavens. I've been asleep for nearly three hours!' she exclaimed as she shoved her arms into the sleeves of her leather jacket. The temperature had dropped quite dramatically.

'You've been snoring your head off.'

Her response was pure outrage. 'I don't snore!'

'Whoever told you that?' he drawled.

'Why…' Grace gritted her teeth. She'd been awake for no more than thirty seconds and already her boss was taunting her. What business was it of his who knew about her sleeping habits? In reality, the number was exceedingly small. But there was no need to share that kind of personal history with a world-class playboy like Mitch Wentworth. 'No one has ever complained about my snoring,' she answered honestly.

Even in the dark interior of the truck's cabin, she could see his eyebrows rise. And his sideways glance was loaded with inference.

With a disdainful sweep of her eyelashes, Grace refused to meet his teasing gaze and turned instead to peer through the window beside her. 'You haven't answered my question,' she said, eyeing the rugged terrain. 'Where are we? What happened to the road?'

'The road's right where it's always been. We're just not following it at the moment.'

This deserved an explanation. Warily, she faced him again. 'But why, for heaven's sake? Have we been through Georgetown?'

Mitch swung the steering wheel sharply to swerve past the rocky outcrop that suddenly loomed in their path. Grace braced herself as, despite her seat belt, she was thrown against the door.

'Sorry about that,' he muttered, once they were safely on the other side. 'To answer your question, we passed through Georgetown over an hour ago. But then I came across a signpost to an old mining site and thought it might be worth taking a look.'

'So you just left the road and took off blindly into the scrub in the middle of the night?'

In the glare of the headlights, she saw the line of Mitch's face stiffen. 'It was still light then and there were clear tracks. And the kind of location I'm looking for is hardly likely to be sitting right next to the highway. I need to be prepared to take a few risks.'

'And has it been worth the detour?'

He shrugged. 'Not really.'

Pounding through the dark along an unknown track in one of the remotest parts of Australia seemed a touch reckless. Grace couldn't resist another question. 'Do you know where we are now? It's so dark you'd be lucky to see a kangaroo hopping straight in front of you, let alone the way back to the main road. I don't fancy spending the night out here.'

'Of course I know where we are. I've turned back. We'll

hit the bitumen again any tick of the clock and you'll be in Croydon in time for a late dinner.'

Grace shivered inside her jacket. She wasn't especially cold, but the grim, deserted landscape and the inky black world beyond the headlights' beam looked menacing. 'This track doesn't look like it's had much use. I'm sorry to keep harping on this. But *how* do you know we're going in the right direction?'

Drawing in a deep, exasperated breath, Mitch glared at her. 'For crying out loud, woman, are you going to question my every move? I was following a good track, but it petered out. Okay? But there are enough signs here for me to follow. We'll be all right. Give me another half-hour, and if we haven't come across the road by then we can rethink our position.'

She clamped her lips tightly shut. In this situation, there was no sense in upsetting Mitch any further, so she sat straight and silent, clutching the safety rail, with her eyes peeled for the first hint of danger ahead. The way was very rough and, to her mind, Mitch was driving too fast. Anthills and boulders seemed to loom suddenly out of the dark and he was forever having to swerve to avoid some kind of hazard. She hoped he wasn't being overly confident just because he had an off-road four-wheel-drive vehicle.

Suddenly the headlights picked up a flash of something ahead. Shadowy black shapes streaked across their path. 'Look out!' she cried, and Mitch slammed on the brakes.

'A mob of wild pigs,' he growled.

The shaggy beasts, some huge and with gruesome tusks, were frightened by the truck's lights and scampered away, squealing and screeching into the murky black world beyond the headlights. Shaken, Grace glanced at Mitch and he flashed her a quick grin. 'How are you holding out there, Ms Robbins? Exciting, isn't it?'

'I think I could do without this kind of excitement,' she replied.

He reached over and tweaked her hair. 'We're not in any danger, Grace,' he said, his voice suddenly gentle. 'We've a sturdy vehicle, plenty of fuel, water and warm clothes. If we have to face the worst and we can't get back onto the road tonight, we can always pull up. You can sleep in here inside the cabin and I'll curl up in the back of the truck.' He leaned over and looked as if he was going to drop a warm kiss on her cheek, but at the last minute changed his mind and straightened again. 'Cheer up. Throw in another CD and let's have some music.'

The truck lurched forward as he accelerated once more and Grace, because she could think of no better suggestion, slipped a CD into the player. In the pitch-dark, she had no idea what she'd selected, but within moments Simon and Garfunkel's soothing voices began to sing the familiar harmonies from the sixties.

And before too long she felt a little better. Mitch was right, she grudgingly admitted. This was a kind of adventure. And if they really had to they could camp out for one night. After last night, she knew she wouldn't have to fight him off. There was no one around and they'd be perfectly safe. It wasn't the wet season, so they weren't in danger of getting bogged or flooded.

She zipped up her jacket, shoved her hands into the pockets of her shorts and wished she were wearing jeans. If she did have to spend the night out here, she would have to change into something warmer.

As their vehicle forged its way through the dark bush, her spirits gradually lifted, and by the time Simon and Garfunkel were singing one of her favourite songs, Grace was relaxed enough to hum along with them. Even if Mitch was a touch devil-may-care, he was a competent driver, she decided. His strong hands held the steering wheel confidently and he changed gears with the ease of a racing car professional.

Even now, as he slipped into a lower gear while they careered around another unexpected mound of boulders, he was completely in control.

Almost!

They both saw it at the same moment.

Before them in the headlights' glare, a gaping, deeply eroded washout cut through the track.

Mitch swore.

There was no chance for him to stop; the channel was far too close and sudden braking would send the vehicle skidding straight down into the deep ditch.

He gunned the motor, knowing his only hope was to jump the truck over the gap. Teeth gritted, he depressed the accelerator and willed the vehicle forward. His heart lurched as the front wheels left solid ground.

He thought they'd made it. But the rear of the truck dipped abruptly, then smashed down into the gully. With a savage jolt, the vehicle crashed to a sickening, sudden halt and ghastly sounds of crumpling metal filled his ears. Mitch's body pitched forward, then the sudden rush and hiss of an inflating airbag burst in his face.

He swore and turned to Grace, who was similarly battling with a safety airbag. 'You okay?' he gasped.

'I think so.'

He heard the clunk and squeak of her door opening and the thud of her feet hitting the ground as she jumped down. Over her shoulder, she called, 'I'll try to see what's happened.'

Mitch grimaced and he punched the airbag in helpless rage. He knew what had happened. A right royal stuff-up! How would he ever urge this vehicle out of such a steep ditch? The motor had stalled, so he reached for the ignition key and flicked it on.

'Hold it!' Grace's sharp cry came from somewhere in the grim darkness outside. 'Wait, Mitch! I think there's a rear wheel torn from its axle. And—and I can smell petrol.'

Frustration had him roaring back at her. 'Stand back! I've got to give it at least one go.'

'No, Mitch, no!'

Ignoring her cries, Mitch turned the ignition key again. He heard the motor try to grind into action. Then everything happened very quickly.

Sparks flashed from somewhere in front of him, followed by the smell of smoke and a muffled explosion.

From a long way off, he heard Grace screaming, 'Mitch! Get out!'

He didn't need a second invitation. Unbuckling his seat belt with frantic fingers, he shoved his door open and dived sideways. With a horrible flaring blast, the truck burst into ugly flames. Mitch rolled across the rocky ground and cleared the conflagration just in time.

Stunned, he lay still on the dirt track for the few short moments it took his mind to catch up with his body. 'Grace?' Where was she? Refusing to notice the cuts and grazes he'd scored, Mitch hauled himself to his feet. All he could see were flames—orange, scarlet and blood-red, disappearing into a cloud of evil-smelling black smoke.

'Grace!' he called again.

And then came the faint reply. 'I'm all right. I'm back here.'

Relieved, he switched his attention to the inferno beside him, and he decided in a flash that there was no way he could just let their only source of transport and shelter burn up!

Desperately, he scraped at the dirt and tossed it towards

the flames. Again and again he tried. But eventually, with a sinking stomach, Mitch had to accept the truth. Even if he had a shovel and a whole mountain of sand, he could not put out that fire.

'Mitch!' Grace called, and he staggered towards the sound of her voice, almost stumbling over her where she sat, huddled beside a boulder.

Feeling dizzy and miserable and several versions of an idiot, he knelt quickly at her side. 'Are you all right?'

'Yes,' she replied in a small voice. 'What about you?'

'I'm okay. Just furious with myself.'

'Furious' wasn't a strong enough word for his sense of rage. He'd just hurtled them headlong into the worst kind of danger. And when Grace had mentioned a petrol smell he should have known that meant the fuel tank was ruptured. Now they were stranded without food, water, warmth or any means of communication.

*In the middle of nowhere.*

Although he'd put on a brave face for Grace, he had absolutely no idea where they were. His head sank into his hands and he groaned aloud.

Her hand patted his shoulder. 'I managed to grab my day pack out of the back of the truck.' Grace held the canvas bag out for him to see.

'Top stuff, Grace.' He sighed. 'You're the only one around here with any brains.' With another groan, Mitch smashed a balled fist against his palm as he looked back at the orange flames engulfing the truck. 'Damn it to hell!'

And once again he felt Grace's cool hand on his wrist. 'It's happened, Mitch,' she said softly. 'There's nothing more we can do. We just have to stay clear-headed now and think this through.'

Mitch closed his eyes and clenched his teeth. This whole mess was his fault. He was surprised that Grace was taking everything so calmly. Now they didn't even have any shelter. *What kind of a boss did that make him?* 'I'm sorry,' he muttered.

She didn't respond. There was another explosion, followed by another flash and a burst of flames from the truck. 'Let's move further away,' Mitch said, and reached down to help Grace to her feet.

They found a couple of flat rocks to sit on and Grace settled her small canvas pack beside her, undid the buckles and began to rummage around inside. 'I'm just checking out all our worldly goods,' she said. After a moment, she turned to him. 'It's not so bad. We have a litre of water, which is pretty important. Two muesli bars, two apples. And…and a map and matches! Thank heavens for that!'

'I didn't even think to grab the mobile phone,' confessed Mitch. He threw his arm around her shoulders. 'I told you this morning, you're magnificent.'

'There's not much else,' Grace replied, apparently ignoring his praise. She was digging down deep and, to his surprise, he heard her giggle. 'Now this is really useful. I've got a spare pair of knickers.'

'You don't say?' In spite of everything that had happened and the mountain of guilt he shouldered, he sensed a totally inappropriate physical response. Mitch forced his voice to sound casual. 'What colour are they?'

And, for some ridiculous reason, Grace laughed. Mitch's shoulders relaxed and his own chortle joined hers. This girl might be uptight and prickly in the office, but when it came to the real crunch she had guts.

After their chuckles subsided, they sat together in the dark with the flickering flames of the wrecked truck lighting up the bush around them. The air was still tainted by the acrid smell of burning rubber.

Mitch's sigh hissed like air escaping from a punctured

tyre. 'I guess we'll have to try to make the best of this,' he said at last. 'At least we can save your matches for now, seeing as we've got this flaming truck barbecue to ignite our timber. I'll see if I can find some wood for a fire. It's going to get quite cool tonight, I imagine. But we may as well stay here till morning and then take stock of our surroundings.'

He built their fire some distance from the burning truck, in the shelter of a small rocky outcrop. When he'd finished, Grace came and sat beside him and they shared one of her muesli bars and had a few sips of water each and stared at the flames. All around them the bush was deathly quiet, so that the only sound they could hear was the snap and crackle of wood burning or, in the distance, the occasional faint howling of dingoes.

'No one knows where we are?' asked Grace.

''Fraid not.'

For the first time, she was frightened. 'When I was asleep, you didn't phone ahead to Croydon?'

'I tried, but the phone wouldn't work. Must be out of the network.'

'So there's no one at all who knows which way we headed after we left Undara?'

'I'm afraid not.' Mitch sighed, and they continued staring at the fire in silence for several minutes before he spoke again. 'Thanks for being such a champion about this. You have every right to lecture me.'

Grace gazed deep into the flames and her lips curled into a self-deprecating smile. It was weird how she could stay so calm in the face of this present danger and yet, at other times, she'd been reduced to a quivering mess by the mere hint of Mitch's awareness of her as a…woman.

'Neither of us is going to drop straight off to sleep,' Mitch added, and Grace found his deep voice a strangely comforting sound filling the silence. 'I guess there's not much for us to do except get to know each other a little better.'

'How do you mean?'

She saw Mitch's grin in the reddish flicker from the fire. 'Calm down, Grace. I'm simply asking you to tell me a bit more about yourself. Tell me about your family.'

Grace drew in a deep breath as she sat with her knees drawn up and her chin resting on them. She switched her gaze from the glowing timbers to the starry sky above, unsure to what extent she wanted to bare her soul to this boss she found so disconcerting. 'Just because we're stranded in the middle of the wilderness, that doesn't mean we have to become bosom buddies.'

Mitch's eyes betrayed his amusement. 'You are exceptionally safe Ms Robbins. We've a long way to go before we reach that point.'

Grace sniffed. 'If you must know,' she replied in a prim, tight little voice, 'I was born on a distant planet and came to earth in a space pod when I was just five centuries old. Two kind earthlings adopted me.' Her glance flicked to Mitch to gauge his reaction.

'That explains a great deal,' he said with a deadpan expression.

'I'm glad to hear it.'

'Now I understand why you're such an intriguing puzzle. I can see that you're superwoman and yet you're afraid of earthmen.' He lay back, linked his hands behind his neck and grinned. 'And you also don't want to talk about your private life.'

'Oh, for heaven's sake,' Grace cried, shaking her head in exasperation. 'Do you have to psychoanalyse me all the time? Okay here come the fascinating details.' She folded her arms across her chest and spoke slowly, her expression flat, as if giving evidence to the police. 'I'm an only child. My parents were fairly old when I was born. I had a very…quiet childhood.' She could have said repressed or boring, but now, in the middle of nowhere with this infuriating man, the safety of home, no matter how dreary, seemed more appealing.

'You were a good student?'

'Oh, yes. I was very studious. Winning prizes on speech night was the best way to please my parents.'

Mitch poked at the fire with a long stick. 'So how did your parents feel when you took a job in the film industry?'

For some reason his question pleased Grace. It made her feel as if he had really listened and was genuinely interested and thinking about what her home life had been like. 'They were devastated at first,' she admitted. 'Especially Dad. He had such high hopes that I would become a doctor or a lawyer or something equally prestigious. But when I was young we never went to the cinema and so—I don't know—maybe I overreacted after all that stifling—but when I first started getting out to the occasional movie as a teenager I was absolutely entranced—totally wrapped. I knew I had to end up involved with them somehow. Mum and Dad eventually got over their disappointment after they saw my name in the credits at the end of the first feature film I worked on.'

'What about the men in your life?'

She sat bolt upright. 'What about them?'

Mitch shrugged. 'Idle curiosity. I know you like to give the impression that you're not interested, but…'

She drew in a breath sharply. Perhaps it would be best if she set him straight right from the start. 'I'm very choosy about men,' she told him quickly, well aware that she sounded nervous.

'Now, why doesn't that surprise me?'

Briefly, she considered mentioning Roger the Rat, but just as quickly she rejected the idea. 'And it works the other way, too. I have limited appeal.' She said this, not daring to look at him as she made her admission. 'I'm too serious and quiet. Men don't find those qualities particularly appealing.'

Mitch was staring at her. His eyes were wide and considering and a faint, sad smile played at the corners of his mouth. 'Not even Henry Aspinall?'

'Especially Henry Aspinall,' Grace responded with a scowl. She leaned forward abruptly. 'That's enough about me. How about you?'

Slowly, he scratched in the dust with a twig. For a long moment he seemed wrapped in his own thoughts, then his head jerked up. 'What was that? My family? My father died when I was ten and my mother had a real struggle to raise my three brothers and me.'

He threw the broken twig into the flames and Grace watched it curl into a blackened crisp. 'My mum wasn't much like your parents, by the sound of it. She wasn't all that interested in academic prizes, but she used to come and watch me play footie...'

'You ended up playing rugby for Queensland, didn't you?'

He looked surprised. 'How on earth do you know that?'

'Oh, I've told you before, I read a lot and I have a good memory.'

Mitch grinned. 'Anyhow, what really pleased my mother was when we boys got part-time jobs that helped to make the dollars go round. For years, I had a paper round and a lawn-mowing service. Later I earned money fixing my mates' computers.' He frowned at Grace. 'Now why are you looking at me like that?'

'Sorry,' she mumbled, ducking her head. Her surprise

must have been showing more than she realised. For some reason she'd imagined Mitch sailing through a comfortable, pampered boyhood, with doting parents to launch him into his brilliant future. 'I'm just coming to terms with the humble beginnings of the famous Mitch Wentworth.'

She watched as he shrugged and smiled. 'If we're doing this fair and square,' she said, waiting for his expression to grow serious again, 'I suppose I should ask you about the women in your life.'

'But you don't need to ask, do you?' The grin lingered. 'I don't?'

'You've already done your research and you know everything there is to know about me. You seem to know, for example, all about my hobbies with women. My habit of going to bed with women I hardly know...'

'I've read what the magazines report. And where there's smoke there's usually...' Grace's cheeks burned as brightly as the flames she stared at, and she lost the necessary confidence to finish her reply. Her boss's private life wasn't really any of her business.

To her relief, Mitch seemed just as keen to let the matter drop. He threw back his dark head and stared up at the sky. 'Just take a look at that. Stars stretching for ever. I've never seen so many.'

Grace followed his gaze. From one distant horizon to the other the great sky curved above them in a huge dome—absolutely crowded with millions of tiny, softly twinkling, silvery stars.

He reached over and gave her a gentle punch. 'And to think some hotels boast about five-star accommodation, Grace. We're beating them hands down tonight.'

She couldn't help smiling back.

His face grew serious again. 'It's a humbling concept—

the vastness of our universe. Have you come to any conclusions about it?'

'It's big?'

Mitch threw back his head and laughed loudly.

'Before you rupture something,' she went on defensively, 'did you know that there are more stars and planets in the universe than there are grains of sand on the beaches of the earth?'

'No.' He laughed. 'I'm afraid that detail had escaped me.'

'I guess you expected something deep and meaningful from me, seeing I claim to be thoughtful and serious,' she amended when his mirth eventually subsided. 'But what I really meant was that the universe is *so* big, that I haven't found any man-made explanation of it all that satisfies me.'

Watching the flames once more, he nodded.

'Actually, we should be able to use the stars to help us work out directions.'

'You think so? I always understood the sun was more reliable. Isn't there some trick you're supposed to be able to do with your watch and the sun?'

Impulsively, Grace leaned over and grasped Mitch's left wrist. An unexpected flash of heat shot through her when she touched him, but she tried to ignore it as she looked at his watch and laughed. 'I doubt a digital watch would be much use. No hands to line up with the compass points.'

'I suppose not,' Mitch agreed. 'I guess the bits and pieces of bushcraft I picked up in my youth are a bit outdated now. So what wonderful little gem of information do you have about direction-finding?'

She stared at the silver speckled sky, searching her memory for exactly what it was she had read. 'I'm sure I've seen somewhere that you can use the Southern Cross. It's somehow connected to the Cross's two pointer stars.'

'What direction does it indicate?'

'Why, south, of course.'

'I would hazard a guess that it was something to do with the line from the long arm bisecting a line drawn through the pointers,' Mitch suggested.

'Yes!' exclaimed Grace. 'I remember now. That's it! That gives you a southerly direction.'

'So, if we follow that point down, we should remember that really tall ironbark over there—the one standing out against the sky—should be more or less south.' Mitch reached out and shook Grace's hand. 'Well done, team.' He held her hand for a moment and stared at her as if he wanted to say more.

Grace's heart jumped. A man lost in the wilderness had no right to look so breathtaking. Somehow, when he was tousled and unshaven, he looked more dangerously attractive than ever.

To her relief, he eased himself backwards so that he lay once more with his hands behind his head, looking up at the huge sky. 'I've just remembered a game we used to play when we were kids. Have a crack at this, Grace. If you were a piece of furniture, what would you be?'

'What *furniture* would I be?' she asked, wondering if he'd banged his head during the smash and was suffering from delayed concussion.

'Yeah,' he urged. 'I know it sounds strange, but it's an interesting exercise. You'll get the hang of it. So, what would you be? A rocking chair, a garden seat?'

'Oh, what the heck?' Grace laughed. 'I'm definitely a mahogany roll-top desk.'

Mitch looked at her and grinned. 'So you are—elegant and immensely practical. And what kind of fruit are you?'

Grace rolled her eyes.

'Fruit? Mitch, I don't know. You must have been an imaginative bunch of kids.'

'I guess we were.'

'I'm probably a…a mango. No, I'm not.' She laughed. 'I'm a slice of perfectly ripe, chilled pawpaw.' Grace shifted onto her side and looked at Mitch as he lay with his handsome profile etched in starlight. The wild, menacing wilderness that surrounded them seemed to diminish and she couldn't help her light-hearted, spontaneous comment. 'And you are a…black sapote.'

'I'm a what?' he asked, turning towards her, his eyes wide with curiosity.

'A black sapote. It's a tropical fruit and it tastes sinfully delicious, like rich chocolate mousse.'

'Am I, now?' mused Mitch. 'I like the sound of that.'

And suddenly Grace was embarrassed, as if she'd let her feelings run away with her. 'But as far as furniture is concerned,' she hurried on, hoping to cover over any unwarranted enthusiasm, 'you'd have to be a…'

'Director's chair?' Mitch asked.

'No. That's far too obvious. No, you're a telephone table.'

He shot her a look of surprise. 'How on earth did you come up with that?'

'Well, you're the boss. You can just stand in hallways and yell and everyone comes running to you.'

Mitch chuckled. 'I can see you're warming to this. Now let me see, if you were a musical instrument, I'd say you'd be a saxophone—playing soft blues or jazz at midnight—sexy, moody and unpredictable.'

*Sexy?* Grace was glad it was dark so he couldn't see the fierce blush that followed his description.

They were back on dangerous ground and an uncomfortable wave of unsettling yearning flooded through her.

This would never do. 'There's no doubt what musical instrument you'd be,' she retorted, her tone more waspish than she'd intended.

'Oh?'

'You'd be a trumpet in a brass band.'

Mitch sighed loudly. 'Now why do I think this sounds like a direct hit at my ego? Do you imagine I'd want to blow my own trumpet as often as I liked?'

'If the cap fits...'

He frowned and levered himself up into a sitting position. 'The party's getting rough. I'm afraid your true feelings are coming out, Ms Robbins.'

Grace was suddenly regretful that she'd been quite so sharp-tongued. Mitch had really been very pleasant company. Overwhelmingly charming company. 'Actually, I was thinking more of what a bright, triumphant sound a trumpet makes,' she suggested, in an effort to make amends.

'Liar,' growled Mitch, but in the firelight his eyes twinkled with good humour. He stood and picked up a log, which he carefully positioned on the fire. 'We can't hope for comfort and we don't know what's ahead of us tomorrow, so how about we try for some rest?'

She nodded, realising how clever he'd been to keep her talking, even laughing. She'd almost forgotten just how serious their situation was.

'You're allowed to snuggle into my back if you get cold,' Mitch said as he settled his long frame down on the ground once more.

'I'll be all right,' Grace murmured. She lay stiffly near the fire and the sharp stones of the surrounding gravel dug into her legs. But as she stared at that big, warm, comforting back she wished desperately that she had more courage. There had never been a back she wanted to snuggle up to more.

# CHAPTER SIX

IT WAS a terrible night.

Grace found trying to keep warm almost impossible. The side of her body away from the fire became bitterly cold, but if she wriggled any closer the heat was unbearably scorching. So she tossed and turned on the hard, unforgiving dirt and felt like a sausage being grilled on a barbecue. And she lay awake for hours, staring at the blinking, distant stars, feeling hungry, thirsty and utterly miserable.

But she wasn't frightened.

She felt strangely confident that they couldn't really be lost. When the sun came up, she and Mitch would get a better look at their surroundings and, with the aid of her map, they'd discover how to get back onto the road. Then it would just be a matter of waiting for someone to drive past. She lay on the hard earth and tried to comfort herself by picturing their rescue.

Mitch slept like the proverbial log. And that didn't help her to cope any better with the long, dark, lonely hours.

When eventually the distant horizon showed the faintest, thin line of pale light, Grace almost wept for joy. Never had she been more relieved to see a new day. And it arrived quite spectacularly, as only an outback sunrise could. Rosy-pink fingers, growing warmer and more deeply hued every minute, spread outward across the huge sky from a brilliant red-gold fingertip of sun. Slowly the burning ball crept higher. No wonder ancient people worshipped the sun, she thought as she watched the enormous glowing circle pulse its triumphant light across the plains.

They breakfasted on a shared apple and a few sips of water. 'I guess this is not very hygienic,' Grace said as she handed Mitch the half-eaten apple and watched his mouth close over it.

The crisp white flesh that had just been in her mouth was now disappearing into his. It was so incredibly intimate—like sharing a toothbrush—the kind of familiar exchange lovers enjoyed.

'You didn't mention any worries about an exchange of germs when I kissed you the other night,' he tossed back at her.

That shut her up and she fumed as he hungrily polished off the fruit—core, seeds, the lot. While he munched, she studied their surroundings.

'Hardly any landmarks worth noting,' Mitch observed gloomily.

Grace had to agree. The Gulf country, which stretched all around them, was almost featureless—flat country with no hills or mountain ranges and covered with sparse scrub and hundreds of red termite mounds.

'We at least have some ideas about direction,' she offered. 'There's our southerly ironbark tree that we noted last night, and I took careful notice of where the sun came up. It was over here. So that's more or less east. North must be this way.' She pointed slightly to their left.

'That's what I was afraid of,' muttered Mitch, and he kicked at a loose stone with his boot and sent it skimming across the hard-baked red earth.

'Afraid?' she echoed. 'Why's that?'

His mouth pulled into a grimly drooping curve as he turned and pointed back towards the burnt-out shell of their truck. 'Look at the way we were heading last night.'

Grace squinted. Beyond the truck, she could make out the faint line of the track weaving its way past termite mounds and scraggy pandanus. Then she looked again towards the point they had determined as south. 'Oh, my goodness, you were driving towards the north,' she said softly. 'Perhaps north-east.'

'When I should have been heading south. South-west, if we were hoping to get to Croydon.' Mitch swore colourfully. 'I can't believe it. How did I end up driving in completely the wrong damn direction?'

Grace bit her lip. Mitch looked so angry with himself and so ashamed, she experienced a flicker of sympathy for her boss. 'Should we look at the map and try to work out where we are?' she asked hesitantly.

He stared at her and his eyes suddenly brightened with their familiar, teasing glint. 'A top-drawer suggestion, Ms Robbins. If you'd be so kind…' With a flourishing gesture, he held out his hand for Grace's map.

She unfolded it and spread it on the ground, so they could both see it. As they crouched in the dirt, Mitch's hand rested lightly on Grace's shoulder so that his fingers, his warm skin, touched hers. She shivered. Didn't he realise what a casual touch like that could do to a girl?

'Here's Georgetown,' she said, trying to ignore the skitters of reaction caused by his proximity. He had hunkered down so close to her that his thigh pressed against her as well. 'Where do you think you left the road?' she asked, a trifle breathlessly.

'About here,' Mitch replied, indicating the spot on the map with his free hand. 'I started heading north, but then I was sure I had turned back to the south.'

'You must have veered off in a bit of an arc and then, without noticing, slowly swung around to the north again,' Grace volunteered.

Mitch rubbed his thumb over his stubble lined chin and fixed her with his dark eyes. Grace drew in a sharp breath.

Fringed by black lashes, his eyes held hers, so that, for a moment, she forgot what they were discussing. Forgot totally that their lives could be in great danger. She was dimly aware that she should have been absolutely panic-stricken! But something much more important was happening. She was drowning in the depths of those beautiful, dark, sensuous eyes.

And, as he squatted in the dirt, he was staring at her as if he'd never seen her before. With a sinking heart, she realised that she probably looked quite terrible. Exhausted and dirty, with no hairbrush, no chance to wash her face—no woman would want a man like Mitch Wentworth to see her in such a state! Self-consciously, she ran her fingers through her hair.

'The wild, untamed look definitely suits you, Grace,' he said softly. 'When we get you back to the office, we'll have to do something about your image.'

With a sickening jolt, Grace came to her senses. 'Will we?' she asked coldly, and she ground her teeth. For a reckless moment there, she had almost allowed herself to think of Mitch as someone other than her boss—as an attractive man. A man she could grow fond of.

What a stupid, stupid mistake. Not only was Mitch Wentworth her boss, he was the Dark Invader. He'd trampled all over poor George Hervey, to forge his way into the company. He was another user, like Roger the Rat.

She wriggled her shoulder away from his touch and stared hard at the map. 'Our chances of ever getting back to the office depend on some pretty careful planning now,' she snapped. 'How long do you think you were driving in the wrong direction?'

'About two hours,' Mitch admitted with a grimace.

'So, taking the rough track into consideration, we're probably about a hundred and fifty kilometres up this way,' Grace suggested. 'About to head up the Cape York Peninsular.'

Mitch squinted as he examined the map once more. 'I'd say you're dead right,' he admitted at last with a deep, weary sigh. They both looked out at the desolate expanse of savannah plain stretching before them. There was no evidence of human existence anywhere. No fence posts, no rooftops, not even a sign of cattle. 'How is anyone going to find us out here? This country is about as remote as it gets.'

'They won't,' Grace told him quietly.

Why didn't she feel more frightened? Their situation was desperate and yet somehow, even though her visit to the outback with the man she'd been determined to hate was turning into a worse nightmare than she could have ever predicted, she felt calm.

Almost safe.

Which was ridiculous given that Mitch didn't look at all relaxed or in control. Resting his elbows on his knees, he buried his face in his hands.

At that moment, a shadow crossed the sun and Grace looked up to see thousands of wild, swift-flying budgerigars free-wheeling across the bright sky. Little specks of green and yellow, they darted and danced agilely through the clear blue space, displaying the careless freedom of creatures who belonged to the natural environment.

Grace followed their movements. *We're alien invaders, out of our element. Displaced. And in great danger of perishing. We have none of the knowledge these wild things share.*

Mitch's hoarse voice invaded her reflections. 'Okay. I'm the boss, and I got us into this disaster. But I've considered our situation carefully and I'll get us out. This is what we've got to do.' He stood up and glared down at Grace, as if challenging her to defy him. His shoulders were squared and his jaw thrust forward belligerently. 'As I understand it, the golden rule when you're bushed is to stay with the vehicle.'

Grace frowned. 'In most circumstances,' she said slowly.

'In every case,' Mitch declared, scowling fiercely. 'It's your only hope of being found.'

'But…' Grace hesitated, and her brows drew low in a deep frown as she puzzled over how to handle this.

'I don't think I could take another of your ''buts'' right now, Grace.' He punched the air in a gesture of defiance and then his hands fell to his hips. He glared at her in angry silence. 'But I'm going to hear it anyway, so fire away.'

Grace rubbed her sweaty hands together nervously and cleared her throat. 'I think that the idea of staying put is very sensible when a car breaks down on a road, or some place where people are likely to come looking for you. Nine times out of ten it would be exactly the right thing to do. But our situation is different. No one—absolutely no one—knows where we are.'

Mitch didn't attempt to interrupt. He just continued to glower at her.

Swallowing, she pressed on. 'We told everyone in the office that we'd be away for five days, so they won't even *begin* to search for us till after that time is up. There's no food or water here, so we can't afford to stay put and just hope. I—I think we might have to work out a way to save ourselves.'

Mitch's hands clenched and he scowled with obvious annoyance, as if he wanted to flick her off the edge of the universe. Then he turned abruptly, marching away from her, his long legs taking enormous strides. Until suddenly, without warning, he spun back dramatically and his face was red—angry, dark red.

He reminded Grace of a cowboy in a shoot-out scene in a third-rate western. She half expected to see Mitch reach for his holster.

'You know what's the matter with you, Grace Robbins?' he bellowed.

'I'm *right*?' she shouted back.

*'EVERY BLASTED TIME!'*

She wanted to yell back at Mitch that he could take a flying leap, but his face suddenly softened into an unexpectedly boyish smile and the words died on her lips. He sauntered back towards her, his hands resting loosely on his hips. His smile lingered. 'Forgive me, Ms Robbins. You're too clever and chock-a-block with common sense for us to fight.' Reaching out, he took her hand. 'Honest, Grace, you're obviously the perfect assistant to be lost with in the outback.'

His gentleness, coming swift on the heels of his attack, floored her. This man sure knew how to calm ruffled feathers. She looked at her hand which had practically disappeared inside his strong grasp. 'If only I was also *willing*,' she muttered, snatching her hand away. And then she grimaced. He'd caught her off guard and now she'd let fly with a hopelessly stupid remark.

'Willing?' Mitch remained standing directly in front of her, a perplexed expression in his eyes as they gleamed from beneath thick lashes.

'Please, forget—forget I said that,' she stammered.

He smiled as he brushed her hair back from her cheek. 'A wild and willing Grace would be an unexpected bonus.' Then his face grew serious again and he dropped his hand to his side. 'But it won't get us out of here.'

There was nothing Grace could think of to say. Her mind was too busy cringing from her stupid gaffe.

'You think we should press on?' Mitch queried.

'We're—um—' Grace cleared her throat. 'We're—um, going to run out of water in less than a day if we stay here.'

Mitch looked again at the map. 'See this development road heading north? I'd say we're about forty kilometres away from it.'

'Yes,' Grace agreed. 'If we try to go back the way we came, we've got at least one hundred and fifty kilometres before we reach a road.'

'So that's settled. We'll push on and follow this northerly track before it gets too hot.'

Although it was mid-winter and the night had been cold, walking for hours under the full strength of the tropical sun soon produced thirst and sweat. Mitch was pleased that Grace could drape her jacket over her head to try to protect her face and bare shoulders from the unrelenting rays. There wasn't the slightest hint of a breeze.

And if they had read the map correctly they had many kilometres to walk. They could run out of food and water before they found the road.

When Grace turned, he was concerned to see how flushed her cheeks were. The symptoms of dehydration flashed through his head: dizziness, fatigue, loss of appetite.

'How much water do we have left?' she asked.

Nervously, he reached into the backpack he was carrying for her and pulled out the clear plastic bottle. 'About half.'

'Mmm. Better save it.'

'No. You have some.'

She didn't wait for a second invitation. 'Just need to wet my whistle,' she murmured, only taking a couple of sips. 'Your turn.'

But Mitch put the bottle back in the pack without taking any. Their lives depended on water, and he could last a little longer. After all, he'd got them into this.

He tried to shrug away the thought. Wallowing in guilt was a useless exercise. But he was very, very worried. Going even a day without water in this heat was perilous. Any longer and they could die. He and Grace wouldn't be the first to come to grief in the unforgiving outback. Australia's history was littered with such stories and, even now, there were tragic news items every year about people who perished terribly from lack of water.

He raised his hand to shade his eyes. 'We need to keep our eyes skinned for any clues that might lead us to water,' he said.

Wearily, Grace looked around her. 'Perhaps we should follow that animal track over there.'

'Perhaps…' mused Mitch. 'But I'd be happier to wait till we found a few more tracks. We need several tracks that are converging to lead us to water.'

She nodded. 'That makes sense.'

'Glad to have your approval, Ms Robbins,' he teased, although his interest in making even the weakest of jokes was rapidly diminishing.

They slogged on, too tired and downhearted to speak… hour followed weary hour.

Hot, tired, thirsty, hungry…

All around them the countryside shimmered under a sun-burnt sky.

Eventually Mitch spoke. 'There's a bit of a ridge over there.' He pointed to their right.

Grace, who had been busy plodding with her head down, hadn't noticed the subtle change in the terrain. She'd been thinking about dying—wondering if she was going to die—out here with her boss. Already she felt weak and dizzy and her mind toyed with the question of whether it was easy to die of thirst. She didn't *want* to die, but what could she do about it? Grace had always imagined she would fight off death with every ounce of her will-power, and she was dismayed to find that now, when she most needed it, her natural determination and fighting spirit had evaporated as quickly as the light dew that had lain on the ground just before dawn.

'We might be able to save our legs and let our eyes do some work if we climb up there and have a good look around.' Mitch's suggestion broke through her cloud of dismal thoughts.

'Good idea,' she muttered, and hurried forward.

Mitch threw out a restraining hand to grab her elbow. 'No need to rush. We've plenty of time. Conserve your energy.'

'Whatever you say.' She was fast approaching the point where she didn't want to think any more. Exhausted and weak, she was quite happy to do as she was told.

When they reached the top of the ridge, the glare of the sun was so strong, Grace couldn't see anything at first. Mitch stood beside her, squinting at their surroundings, offering no comment. She rubbed a grimy hand over her eyes. 'What can you see?'

When there was no response from Mitch, Grace used her hands to shade her eyes and examine the view for herself. Her heart thumped. 'Oh, my... Oh, thank goodness,' she breathed.

They were standing on the top of an escarpment—a red slash of rock dropped down to a huge platform. And in the middle of the platform was a large pool of water carved out of the rock. Fringed by scraggy pandanus palms, no water had ever looked more wonderful.

Below that, there was another rocky drop. In the wet season, a waterfall would tumble over it to the plains below.

Mitch's voice was hesitant. 'You see what I see? It's not a mirage?'

Grace watched a black and white ibis dive into the pool, sending out circling ripples. 'No, it's not a mirage. It's—it's—oh, Mitch, we're not going to die. It's water! *It's water!*'

'We've been walking on a plateau.'

'And that's the coastal plain down there. And we've found *water*!'

'Eureka!' shouted Mitch, his eyes shining. He snatched up Grace in an excited hug and his arms welded her against his heated body. And, suddenly, she was shaking with silly tears springing into her eyes. It was exhaustion, of course—and aftershock.

Last night, when they had faced immediate danger, she'd been calm and in control. Now, when they'd found life-saving water and shade—maybe even food—Mitch's little show of jubilation was making her tremble like a frightened bandicoot.

He frowned at her and, with a lean finger, traced the path of a tear down her dust-streaked cheek. 'You've been incredibly brave,' he said gently. 'Just hold on for a little longer.'

Grace had never been so grateful of manly support. She sank against Mitch and his arms held her close, his chin resting on the top of her head. Hot, tired and dusty, she relaxed against his strength. How firm and strong he felt. His hand was stroking the back of her neck, slowly, soothingly.

She might have stayed there, relishing the sense of comfort and strength he gave, if her body hadn't betrayed her. Mitch's gentle touch kick-started every womanly part of her.

Never before had she been so acutely conscious of just

how perfectly a man's hard muscles complemented a woman's yielding softness. The effect of the pressure of his lower body, tight against hers, caused her to wonder what she'd been doing all her life. Why hadn't any other man ever made her feel this sudden sunburst of wild longing?

She was quite definitely affected by the heat, she decided.

The heat—and the shock of her boss, Mitch Wentworth, handing out tenderness. They were a heady combination. No wonder she was a shivering mess.

Grace stiffened in his embrace and her chin lifted. 'Er... excuse me, Mr Wentworth,' she said primly. 'But you seem to have your arms around me.'

'Pardon?' Mitch looked puzzled. But he let her go quickly, both arms flinging wide. Grace felt his withdrawal more acutely than she would have liked.

'We have a deal,' she said unsteadily. 'No close encounters of the physical kind, except on request. Remember?'

His dark gaze locked with hers and Grace's throat constricted. In Mitch's eyes, shock and disbelief warred with something that must surely be contempt.

She looked away.

'Caught out on a technicality,' he drawled, before letting out a heavy sigh. Then he shook his head and released a half-hearted laugh. 'Okay. Let's take it slowly climbing down these rocks. We don't want to have an accident at this stage.' He shot her a wary glance. 'You might need to allow me to take your hand for the really steep bits.'

Luckily, their journey down the cliff was not too difficult. Although the orange sandstone was worn smooth, there were still footholds, carved over the centuries by wind, sand and water and, at times, they could hang onto the strong roots of fig trees which, miraculously, clung to the rock wall.

And Grace allowed Mitch to help her over the really difficult sections. With eyes downcast, she muttered her thanks.

When, at last, they reached the safety of the rocky platform, Grace stepped forward eagerly. The pool was cool, clear and sparkling. At one end it came hard up against the sandstone bluff and in the middle it spread out and formed a little curving shallow bay where lily pads floated serenely. In an overhanging branch, black cockatoos with their bright red flashes chattered while they kept guard.

Eden could not have looked more pristine or untouched. More inviting.

She dragged off her boots and rushed into the water fully clothed. The cockatoos and a pair of ibises took off with a wild flapping of wings.

And after tossing the backpack aside, Mitch followed her. Splashing and frolicking, they drank the clear, life-giving water with cupped hands like happy children on holidays.

'What's the verdict?' Mitch called, after his dark head, wet and sleek, surfaced some distance away.

'It's amazing.' She laughed back at him. 'If only we had food, I could settle in here.'

With slow, leisurely strokes, he swam closer. 'Don't talk about food,' he moaned. 'You'll set me fantasising about a sizzling, juicy barbecued steak.'

'With jacket potatoes,' added Grace, licking her lips.

'Pan-fried mushrooms.'

'A garden salad and a bread roll, fresh from the oven.'

'Stop it, woman!' groaned Mitch. 'A few minutes ago I was happy with water, but now I'm starving. Heck, I'm so ravenous I could eat a horse and chase the rider.'

'And for dessert there'd be hot apple crumble and—'

Grace didn't get to finish the sentence. Using his big hands as paddles to scoop up the water, Mitch started to swamp her mercilessly with a man-made tidal wave. 'Help!' she cried, gasping and laughing simultaneously. 'Stop splashing!'

'Do you promise to stop talking about food?'

'Yes.'

His hands stilled and Mitch stood knee-deep in the water facing her, laughing, panting, every line of his strongly muscled body outlined by the wet clinging shirt and jeans. Grace tried to drag her eyes away, but he was so darned beautiful. She stood there, drinking in each trim and taut detail.

And he was staring at her, too.

With a start, she realised that her body was even more distinctly revealed. Her stretch-knit top was every bit as wet and clinging as his clothes. She might as well be naked.

She folded her arms across her chest.

Slowly, Mitch waded towards her. When he was level, he paused. 'I'll stop looking at you, if you'll stop checking me out,' he said softly, a little breathlessly. 'Otherwise we'll end up back in the danger zone. Your no-go territory.'

Too late, Grace flicked her gaze away and, while her cheeks blazed, she made a pretence of studying the bright blue backdrop of sky.

'I made you a promise, Grace, but you've got to help. You can't look at a man like you want to peel his clothes off.' A puzzled smile hovered, lightening his gaze, twitching at his lips. 'Do you know what you want, Grace Robbins?'

'I certainly know what I *don't* want!' she bit back. She didn't want this growing need to touch him. And she certainly didn't want this strong desire to experience his touch, the comfort of his arms holding her, the tender thrill of his kiss.

His smile faded. 'Bully for you.'

'Actually,' she continued, with a defiant little lift of her chin, 'I haven't finished talking about food.'

'You don't say?'

'There's got to be food here, Mitch. You know—bush tucker. There's plenty of bird-life around. Perhaps there's fish?'

He nodded, surveying the pool through squinted eyes. 'And the holidays I spent in the bush when I was young might just come in useful after all.'

They lunched on the last shared muesli bar. Mitch stripped off his shirt and hung it over a nearby branch to dry. Grace sat on a rock with her back to that broad, bronzed body and she was grateful that the sun quickly dried her clothes. Afterwards, she decided to curl up in the shade of a clump of pandanus and rest. Sleep was what she needed and she didn't want to think about Mitch, or the possibility of finding the development road. She couldn't even bring herself to worry about food. She was completely exhausted.

Mitch watched her, curled in the shade, long lashes resting against the soft, slightly sunburnt curve of her cheek and her hair streaming out on the rock behind her. Her lissom loveliness was gut-wrenching.

But he knew this was no Sleeping Beauty lying around waiting for her prince to come. Grace Robbins would decide exactly when she wanted a man. And then she would have a detailed list of criteria the poor fellow would need to meet. No doubt she would put him through a series of stringent, secret tests.

She was just like those fairy-tale princesses, he decided, wryly acknowledging that only a movie maker with his head in the clouds would come up with such a comparison. She kept herself locked up tight in a tower. A tower made up of her own very clear expectations.

He remembered the sexy goddess in black lace, framed by Henry Aspinall's doorway, and frowned. Clearly Grace wrote her own rules—and broke them when it pleased her.

And the fact that he, Mitch Wentworth, wouldn't get past the first rung of any ladder leading to her tower was damned annoying.

# CHAPTER SEVEN

GRACE was hungry.

It was late in the day when she woke to gnawing hunger pangs. The rock where she slept was still warm from the sun, but the trees' shadows had lengthened—reaching across one end of the rock pool, making the water look dark and cool.

She struggled to remember how much they had left to eat. One apple! Heavens above, she didn't think she could last another night without more food than that. Where was Mitch? came her next thought.

A pair of rock wallabies moved soundlessly in a lazy, leisurely lope across the terrace. After they disappeared, heading down to the grassy plains below, she rose to her feet and scanned the area. Quite an assortment of birds seemed to be taking their evening drink at the rock pool. Dozens of small finches with bright rosy beaks and brilliant red blazes across their rumps were perched along the sandstone rim. They took dainty sips of water and tilted their heads back to swallow.

Not wanting to disturb them, Grace sat very still and continued to survey the area. Her forehead wrinkled in surprise. Mitch had been busy. A huge heap of firewood was piled on a sandy 'beach' at the edge of the little bay.

Eventually the birds left and she stood and wandered around the rocky platform that skirted the pool's perimeter. Her hair flapped about her face as a late afternoon breeze flicked it playfully. Next to the wood pile rested an old, blackened billycan. Where on earth had Mitch found that?

She looked around her, uneasy that she couldn't see him, and walked to the edge of the water, wondering if he was fishing or perhaps diving. Boy, she was hungry! In the water below her lay an unusual bundle of twigs held down by a rock. Frowning and curious, she stepped into the water, rolled the stone away with her toe and pulled the clump of twigs out. A sharp jab of pain shot through one finger. Screaming, she dropped the sticks.

'Grace, what is it?' From somewhere behind her, Mitch came running. He was slightly breathless when he reached her and grabbed her shoulders. 'Are you all right?'

'Something *bit* me.' She sucked at her throbbing finger, absurdly pleased by the concern evident in his expression.

'What was it?'

'I don't know. It was in that pile of sticks.'

'Oh.' Mitch's glance fell to the twigs she had dropped. A flicker of exasperation darkened his features. He reached down and, grasping the bundle carefully at one end, lifted it out of the water and examined it. 'Good one. I'd say you've just lost our dinner.'

'Our dinner? Oh, no! I couldn't have!'

''Fraid so. I'd say we had a crayfish in there. And this *pile of sticks* you just tipped upside down and destroyed was my carefully engineered, highly scientific crayfish trap.'

'You designed that bundle of sticks?'

'Of course I designed it. It's bushcraft perfected. And this trap has to be picked up very carefully or our precious meal gets clear away.' He muttered a soft curse. 'A fat, juicy freshwater crayfish would have been rather tasty roasted over the coals.'

'Ohh and I'm so hungry,' she moaned. 'How was I to know? It didn't look much like a trap.' Grace shrugged guiltily and pulled a grimacing face. 'But I'm sorry. Trust me to lose our dinner!'

Contrite, she watched Mitch shake his head as he spoke. 'What do they say about women and their relentless curiosity?'

A hot retort formed on her lips, but Grace managed to remain silent. At this particular point in time, hunger was more important than worn-out sexist battles.

Mitch's lips were also tightly clamped as he busily rearranged his trap. Grace watched as he retied one end of the sticks with a length of grass.

'What's that nut thing you're putting inside?'

'A crushed pandanus nut. That's the bait.'

'Oh, I see. So the crayfish crawls down this kind of funnel?'

'Yeah.'

'Do you think he's dumb enough to try it a second time?'

He lowered his trap into the water again and flashed her a brief grin as he repositioned the stone to weigh it down. 'I don't have much info on the IQ of the freshwater crayfish. I guess we'll just have to hope it's not too high.'

'I know that the memory span of a goldfish is three seconds.'

Mitch folded his arms across his chest and laughed. 'And I guess you read that somewhere.'

Grinning foolishly, Grace rubbed at her arms as the early evening breeze gusted over them. She knew they could expect the temperature to drop quite quickly as soon as the sun went down. 'You've collected plenty of firewood.'

'Yeah.' He nodded. 'We'll be more comfortable tonight. I remembered how the Aborigines do it. They build three fires and leave plenty of space to sleep in the middle.'

'To avoid scorching on one side and freezing on the other?'

His grin flowed over her. 'We'll be warm as toast.'

She gulped and dismissed thoughts of lying near Mitch on the soft sandy beach, clean from a swim in the rock pool and warmed by three fires. 'We'll be warm but hungry, thanks to me.'

He didn't answer that. 'I'll start building a fire here. Do you want to make one over there?'

Hoping to redeem herself after losing their meal, Grace built her fire very carefully, starting with small twigs and sticks and gradually adding bigger pieces of timber until she had a neat, solid-looking pyramid.

At last she looked up from her work. Mitch had built the other two fires, his methods more slapdash. Grace studied the stark differences between their efforts—his timber piles were thrown together with a kind of casual, rustic elegance and her trim, geometrically accurate affair looked ridiculously neat. She sighed.

When would she ever learn not to be so fussy?

Mitch eyed her handiwork with ill-concealed amusement and she was grateful he didn't take the opportunity to make fun of her. 'We'll use your fire as the cooking fire, and keep the others for warmth later on,' was all he said.

'How long will it take for the crayfish to try the bait again?'

He cocked his head to one side as if calculating his answer carefully. 'Better give him another hour. But we can always eat water lily tubers. They're supposed to be quite okay. Would you like to dig some up and boil them in this billy I found?'

'Yeah, sure thing,' she replied offhandedly, not prepared to admit that she didn't know how. *She didn't even know water lilies had tubers!*

Mitch tossed her the billycan and then strode off to the

far side of the rock pool whistling an annoying, jaunty little tune.

Luckily, after she rolled her shorts up high and re-entered the water, Grace discovered that the tubers were exactly where one might expect them to be—at the base of the water lily plant. Pulling them up out of the mud was more difficult. They were very deeply embedded in the heavy silt in the bottom of the pool, but they came away eventually when she tugged with all her strength. Except that, as they finally left the clinging, squelchy silt, the force sent her tumbling backwards into the water.

'Darn it!'

Mitch returned at that moment to find her dripping wet, yet again, and floundering around in the shallows, trying to pick up the precious tubers she'd dropped as she'd collapsed. 'I'm okay!' she yelled at him before he could comment.

It was almost dark, and she couldn't see what he was carrying, but his arms were full. He seemed to shrug his acknowledgement and continued on towards the fire. With her bare toes, Grace located the smooth bulbs she'd dropped. She would never have forgiven herself if she'd lost their second course as well as the first.

By the time she'd washed the muddy tubers and filled the billycan with fresh water, Mitch had the fire started and was squatting in front of it. She shivered as she placed her contribution to the meal on the rock beside him.

Over his shoulder, his gaze assessed her. 'You're cold. You'd better get out of those wet things.'

Grace stiffened and her tongue seemed glued to the roof of her mouth. 'I—I'll be all right,' she muttered at last. Did he think she'd had a sudden personality transplant? There was no way she could strip off and parade around naked in front of him. 'The fire will soon dry me.'

'Not fast enough in this chilly night air,' he growled impatiently. Standing quickly, he tugged his shirt out of the waist of his jeans. The movement exposed a shadowing of hair that tapered down from his chest and turned Grace's insides to jelly. 'Here, wear this for a while. And we'll dry your clothes at one of the other fires.'

Despite her best intentions, Grace couldn't help staring as his well-developed shoulders, tinged ruddy by the fire-light, emerged from the shirt. Soon the broad chest was fully exposed. And for Grace the cooling night air wasn't a problem at all. A heatwave was swamping her.

Flustered, she found the words to issue a protest. 'There's no need for you to give up your shirt. I have my leather jacket.'

Mitch tossed her the shirt. 'You can wear your jacket if you like, but it won't cover much.' He shrugged and grinned. 'Not that I would raise any objections.'

Grace pulled a face. He was dead right about the jacket. It was waist-length—hopelessly short.

'Now get over there behind the trees and get changed before I take those wet clothes off for you,' Mitch ordered.

She scurried obediently off into the dark grove of trees, quite certain that it was exasperation and not amusement that caused the fiery gleam in Mitch's eyes.

As she peeled off her wet shorts, she began to wish that she weren't so uptight about Mitch Wentworth. Here she was, stranded with him in the outback in the kind of clichéd fantasy situation most girls dreamed about. She should be deliriously excited. She was alone with a man whose looks alone could have won him the lead in a string of top-billing movies.

She wriggled out of her wet shirt. But he was her boss, for heaven's sake! An annoying, arrogant, pig-headed boss, she reminded herself. A devastatingly handsome, *bachelor* boss, another part of her brain argued.

Grace could imagine her workmate Maria's scornful expression when she heard that she had been alone in the bush with Mitch and had behaved like a terrified schoolgirl. Bare-breasted and shivering, she fished around in her backpack for the spare pair of knickers.

Something in the backpack moved.

Something round and smooth and long.

And *slithery*.

She dropped the bag. Screamed and screamed again, as she catapulted out of the trees. *'Snake! Help, Mitch! It's a snake!'*

He was beside her in a moment, holding a flaming branch above him like a torch.

'Did it bite you?'

She shook her head.

'Where is it?' he asked quickly.

Shuddering, Grace pointed to the grove of pandanus. 'In there. In my p-pack.'

Warily, with the burning torch in front, Mitch edged forward. 'I can see it. It's trying to get away as fast as it can. It's as frightened as you are, Grace, and it's out of your pack now and climbing that tree.' He stepped closer.

'Leave it alone! Keep away from it!' she shrieked.

'It's okay. It's a python!' He turned and grinned at her. 'It isn't deadly. Quite harmless.'

She stood behind him, her hands still shaking, desperately trying to hide her topless state. How was it that fate had delivered her, once again, into a situation that found her parading nearly naked in front of Mitch Wentworth?

'If we leave the snake alone and stay over by the fire, it will leave us alone.'

'You're—you're sure?'

'Absolutely. The dangerous ones don't climb trees.' He sent her another reassuring smile and his gaze dropped to her chest, but just as quickly he flicked his eyes back to his torch.

'M-my clothes,' she stammered as she tried, ineffectively, to simultaneously point at the abandoned huddle of garments and cover herself with her hands. 'They're—they're in there.'

'Okay. Keep your hair on. I'll get them for you.' Mitch rescued the backpack and his shirt, then went back for her wet clothes.

There was no way she would go back into the grove to change. She turned her back to Mitch. It didn't help that as she dragged his shirt over her head it smelled faintly of smoke and heated male. Its sleeves hung out over her hands and the tails finished halfway down her thighs. At least it covered her.

Grace felt calmer as she rolled the sleeves back, while Mitch discreetly carried her wet clothes over to the second fire he had lit, and spread them out on the rock to dry. She knew enough about snakes to know that Mitch was right. They would be perfectly safe if they stayed by the fire.

Mitch returned to crouch over his cooking. All around them, beyond their glowing fires, Grace could sense the silent, night-black bush reaching out to the distant, starry horizons.

They might have been the only two people on the planet.

'Why is it that women always look so much better in men's shirts than guys do?' he asked as she self-consciously made her way back to him. He poked casually at the coals with a long piece of wire and his gaze rested on her with unexpected appreciation as she neared him.

Tamping down the heady scamper of pleasure his words brought, she tried to ignore his gaze. 'I guess at least half the population, the female half, might not agree with you.' She wrinkled her nose and sniffed the night air hungrily as her growling stomach told her that something smelled *good*. 'What are you cooking?'

'Crayfish.'

'Wow! So the fellow I lost crawled back into your trap?' He stood up. 'Actually, no.'

'But…how did you catch him?'

'Catch *them*,' he corrected.

'Excuse me?'

'The five other traps I set all worked famously. We're going to have a feast.'

Her jaw dropped open and she levelled a swift punch at Mitch's upper arm. 'You mean to say you set *five other traps*? And you didn't tell me? You beast! You let me think I'd lost our one and only chance for a feed? You *pig*!' She let fly with another right hook. Mitch didn't flinch. Grace did. His arm was as solid as a block of concrete and her hand hurt.

'You can't expect to know everything, Grace,' he drawled.

She sniffed haughtily and dropped to her haunches, making a pretence of examining the fire and her water lily tubers as they simmered in the billycan. She needed to concentrate on the food and forget about the obnoxious man and his beautiful, bare-chested body standing right behind her.

But the next moment he was crouching right beside her. Startled to find he'd moved so close, Grace nearly pitched forward into the fire.

'These shouldn't take very long.' Apparently unaware of her tension, Mitch rolled a crayfish over with the piece of blackened wire that he'd found.

'How will we break them open?' Her stomach was doing

somersaults and she told herself it was the tempting aroma of roasting crayfish that caused the sensation.

'One thing I do have in my jeans is my trusty pocket knife,' Mitch informed her with a wide grin. He handed the knife to her. 'Here, give those lily bulbs a poke and see if they're cooked. I thinks our crays are ready.'

Everything was ready.

'Gourmet food in the bush.' Mitch grinned as he handed Grace her meal of succulent white crayfish and sliced water lily tubers on a strip of pandanus leaf.

If the smell was tantalising, the taste was pure heaven. 'Mmm…yummo,' she mumbled between mouthfuls.

They munched in the happy silence of people who had been truly hungry. But after he'd polished off two of the crayfish and half the tubers Mitch began to chat companionably. He brought up a range of topics, and Grace was surprised to discover that they both adored rainy days and loved reading autobiographies. And they shared a penchant for visiting museums, while they both hated pizza with too much cheese.

Grace revealed that she had an ambition to one day make a romance movie set in Thailand—an idea that intrigued Mitch. And he outlined for her his dream to eventually create a film about his great-grandmother, who had lived a life of incredible hardship, danger and courage as an early Australian outback pioneer.

And slowly, as Grace's hunger pangs diminished, the world began to seem a whole lot brighter.

'We've been very lucky.' Mitch's smile was wide, as if his own spirits were also lifting. He wiped sticky fingers on a piece of pandanus. 'We have food, shelter, water and warmth.'

'We just need to be rescued now.'

He looked at her sharply. 'You're in a hurry to be rescued?'

'Of course. Aren't you?' she asked, while her heart gave a strange little lurch.

'I guess so,' he said ambiguously as he broke open the last crayfish. 'But I don't know. I could do with a few days of enforced isolation in a remote little Eden like this. Life's pretty hectic out there in the real world. I rather fancy the idea of no deadlines. No phone calls...' He grinned again. 'We've got everything we want here—and, unlike in the movies, no one is shooting at us.'

Grace couldn't take her eyes from Mitch. He looked so happy, so relaxed and at peace with his simple surroundings—and amazingly sexy with his dark, rumpled hair and his eyes reflecting the fire's glow. And, if she were really honest, she had to admit that with each moment she spent alone with him he seemed to grow less and less like the bossy jerk she'd once thought him to be.

In fact, apart from his looks, he seemed to have very little in common with her old boyfriend, Roger. There had always been selfish elements to Roger's personality. But Mitch had been rather thoughtful...respecting her needs... keeping her spirits high...protecting her...

He was still smiling at her now and she sensed a happy glow beginning to make her feel fuzzy from the toes up.

A weird kind of excitement bubbled through her, as if something wonderful might be about to happen. It was just like the first time she'd sat in the movies, her nostrils filled with the hot, salty smell of popcorn while she'd perched on the edge of her seat and watched the heavy velvet curtains draw back.

Happiness swirled and floated all the way up through her body, till she was filled to the brim with a trembling sense of expectation.

The realisation hit her with the force of a meteor slamming into Earth. She *wanted Mitch to kiss her*! Needed him to kiss her.

Grace stopped eating. Perhaps she'd stopped breathing; she couldn't tell. All she knew was that this warm welling of emotion, this sudden longing for Mitch Wentworth, seemed to be the only right and certain thing in the universe.

She couldn't drag her mind away from how nice he'd been to her. She couldn't tear her eyes away from the way the fire highlighted his masculine beauty, creating sexy shadows, angles and planes.

And he was looking at her as if he sensed the reason for her sudden stillness. Could he hear the frenetic pounding of her heart? Her ragged breathing? What could she do about this dilemma? For Pete's sake, she had issued instructions that this man was not to touch her! And now she couldn't think of anything she wanted more than for him to take her into his arms.

She wanted to be held against that strong chest. She wanted to rest her cheek against that smooth shoulder while her nose and mouth nuzzled that brown neck. Most of all, she wanted to have his lips seek out hers.

This was so ridiculous! If she wanted him to kiss her, she would have to ask him. *Out loud!*

Her cheeks flamed as she pushed the empty crayfish shells aside and inched her bottom across the sand just a tiny notch closer to Mitch. The night air zinged with her tension and he didn't move a muscle; he didn't speak.

But he was looking straight at her.

The world around them grew very still and absolutely quiet—as if every stick and star, each rock and tree had become tense and taut in sympathy with Grace's longing.

Even the fire seemed to have stopped crackling.

Silence…silence…silence.

The night was so very hushed that Grace could not raise her voice above a whisper. 'I was wondering…' she mumbled.

Mitch leaned his glossy dark head a little closer to catch her words.

Breathless, she stared at the bronze curve of his shoulder and took a deep, heart-thumping breath. 'I was wondering if you might consider—' Oh, why was she so nervous? She was shaking. She couldn't do this.

'What was that, Grace? Consider?'

'Yes,' she squeaked.

'Consider what exactly?'

'Would you consider…?' Grace knew that if she looked into Mitch's eyes she would find them teasing her. So she stared instead at his strong and comforting chest. 'Consider breaking our contract. Do you *think*? Might you give some *thought*…?'

Closing her eyes, she cursed her exasperating shyness. This was absolutely the wrong way to go about seduction. She was way too tense. Any other girl would have flirted and joked with Mitch and together they would have 'fallen into' a kiss naturally and spontaneously, the way it happened in the movies.

The way it happened for every other couple in the whole world.

When she opened her eyes, Mitch was still waiting quietly and he was staring at her. He seemed to be taking deep, difficult breaths.

She realised she'd waited far too long to even try to finish her question. And now, when he looked at her like that—as if he was as tense as she was—there was no way she could find the words she needed. 'I'll rinse out the billy,' she blurted instead, and, grabbing the can, dashed to the edge of the rock pool.

She crouched on the sandy edge and noisily sloshed water into the billycan, breaking the watery reflection of the starry sky into tiny spots of dancing light while she willed herself to calm down.

For crying out loud, how could a woman of twenty-six have so much difficulty asking a man for a simple kiss? Could it have something to do with the fact that there was nothing simple about her boss's kisses? She felt a cringe of embarrassment as she remembered how she'd made such an almighty fuss last time he'd kissed her. Or perhaps it was that a kiss out here, between a man and a woman alone in the wilderness, would almost certainly lead to much, much more?

That thought had her jumping to her feet and shaking out the excess water from the billy. Nervously, she watched the ripples spread and flatten and she wondered what Mitch was thinking of her strange behaviour.

Her answer came with the slight crunch of footsteps in the sand behind her. Hairs lifted on the back of her neck. And her breath caught as his hands came to rest lightly on her shoulders.

Slowly his thumbs massaged her. 'Are you running away from me?'

She felt her shoulders being drawn back to rest against his warm, bare chest and shivers chased each other down her spine. Mitch's voice murmured in her ear. 'Were you wanting to ask me something, Grace?'

She nodded and he leaned even closer so that his stubble grazed her cheek. 'You were asking me to give some thought…'

Her body burned out of control. Shaking, she turned in his arms and his hands adjusted to the shift, still holding her against him. This man was absolutely irresistible and there was no longer anything she could do about it.

Her next words came of their own accord. 'I—I want you to kiss me.' Overcome by her temerity, her eyes flew shut.

And when he didn't answer she felt terrible. *Mitch didn't want to kiss her.*

Grateful for the darkness, Grace could feel blushes of embarrassment burning her cheeks. Her mind cringed. Mitch had kissed the world's sexiest women. Why would he want to kiss her? How could she ever have…?

Her frantic thoughts were invaded by the touch of a hand on her cheek.

She could feel Mitch's knuckles tracing twin lines from her ears to her lips. Her eyes shot open and he opened his hands to capture both sides of her face. And when she looked up Grace found in his gaze the same wild hunger she was feeling.

'You have the very best ideas, Grace Robbins,' he murmured. 'I don't think I've ever heard a suggestion that has interested me more.' His belt buckle nudged her stomach provocatively. 'I've been giving plenty of thought to kissing you.'

Unable to answer, she simply nodded.

And she trembled as his lips lowered towards hers. His warm, persuasive mouth roamed temptingly over Grace's parted lips and she released a tell-tale, eager little gasp. His hands shifted to her buttocks, lifting her tight against his hardness, while his tongue delved deep in her mouth, questing and promising, sending a slow-burning, languorous flame all the way through her.

She moaned softly, growing giddier, hotter, more carefree…more powerful than she'd ever felt before.

Queen of the Night.

Turning to liquid.

Floating on a cloud of heat.

It was a kiss she never wanted to end.

So when it did stop, when Mitch lifted his head, she felt robbed of something vital—like her lungs. He looked down at her from beneath heavy, lowered lids. 'I knew you were just as good at kissing as you are at everything else, Grace.'

Then why did you stop? she wanted to cry. She swallowed back a painful lump of disappointment. 'Will—will I need to offer an invitation for every kiss?'

'Oh, so you'd like more?'

*She might die if there were no more!*

She lifted her fingers to his lips and his eyes burned into hers as he kissed each finger slowly, one by one. Dreamily, she moved her hand higher and gasped as he licked the trembling palm. The feel of his tongue against her skin sent another molten wave of longing tumbling low inside her.

'No doubt about it, Mitch, I want more,' she whispered shakily.

'Thank heavens for that,' he growled. And, pulling her savagely against him, he crushed her mouth with a kiss that was as urgent as it was seeking, his lips and tongue totally wild as if he couldn't get enough of her.

# CHAPTER EIGHT

MITCH knew they should have piled green leaves on their three fires to make three white plumes of smoke. That was the best way to send a distress signal in the remote outback. Any plane flying overhead would spot it and know at once that it was an SOS call.

But when the sun rolled over the horizon the next morning he had no thoughts of drawing attention to their plight. He didn't particularly want to be rescued. He lay watching the pink and grey streaks of another new day stretch across the heavens, and enjoyed the warmth of Grace's cheek as it rested against his shoulder.

With his finger, he traced the outline of her ear as she slept. This woman sure was a surprise package. Who would have known that being in the wilderness would strip every uptight, prim mouthed and pedantic little habit from her psyche, leaving her warm and lovely and totally unrestrained?

The thought of taking her back to the office and risking the chance that she would slip back behind the old, crusty camouflage was too depressing to consider.

Grace stirred against him, and her green eyes opened slowly. 'Good morning.' She smiled and, turning in his arms, she pressed her mouth to a hollow at the base of his throat.

Mitch groaned. To hell with planning a rescue!

He bent to taste Grace's sleepy, pouting lips and a low, growling sound rumbled in his throat. To hell with business. What could a man do when such a lovely woman stretched out her soft, feminine curves so temptingly beside him? For Pete's sake, who cared about budgets, or the clamour of casting agencies? He wanted to forget the pressure of projected deadlines. Surely losing himself in this woman was all that mattered.

'I think we should spend at least another day here before we push on,' he told Grace much later, after their morning dip in the pool. 'We need to recover from—our ordeal.'

She smiled a shy, knowing little smile, but she didn't object. And Mitch was happier than he had been for a long, long time.

They made the most of their day—capering like silly children in the sun-warmed water, laughing together as they collected more crayfish and water lily bulbs, or discussed their favourite movies and argued about those they hated.

And, more than once, they made love. Circled by clusters of ferns, the patch of green couch grass growing in the deep shade of the pandanus clump was, in Mitch's opinion, as romantic as any plush hotel suite.

And, at the end of the day, there was another night with Grace under the big outback skies and the silent vigil of a million stars.

But as the next morning dawned, Mitch had to face hard facts. They couldn't stay out here for ever. It was time to leave their sanctuary, even though the urge to hide from civilisation for even just a little longer was overwhelming.

His breath expelled on a long, heavy sigh. The old adage 'Time is money' was all too true. And, with most of his own personal fortune invested in the *New Tomorrow* project, money was a vital commodity. Rubbing his hand across the unfamiliar stubble of his four-day-old beard, Mitch knew that he couldn't afford to take too many business risks.

'We really should set off again today.'

Grace turned away quickly to hide her disappointment. She knew Mitch was right, but wondered if he hated the idea of leaving as much as she did.

'By my calculations,' Mitch continued, 'the road is only about another twenty to twenty-five kilometres away.'

'So we should have our breakfast, fill up our bottle as well as the billycan with fresh water, and head off towards the road,' she said, forcing any nuance of disappointment out of her voice.

'Once we reach the road, we're sure to be picked up.'

All morning, as they walked, clouds piled on the horizon in big, fluffy grey heaps.

'With a bit of luck, we'll get a storm this afternoon,' Mitch commented as, towards midday, they trudged across the coastal plains country.

'It would certainly be nice to get some relief from all this humidity,' Grace agreed.

He ran his sleeve across his brow, and then pointed some distance ahead. 'We should take a break when we get to that bunch of eucalyptus trees over there. It makes sense to spend the hottest part of the day resting in the shade.'

'I know all about you and what your idea of a rest in the shade entails, Mitch Wentworth.' She sent him a sultry, playful little smile.

He grinned back at her. 'I'm only thinking of what's best for you. It's common sense in the Tropics to take a siesta.'

A siesta with Mitch in another shady grove! Grace smiled again and prickles of pleasure broke out everywhere. How on earth had it happened that she was constantly thinking about making love when she was virtually lost in the middle of nowhere? Mitch had turned her into a wanton woman.

As her mind tussled with the challenge of finding a smart

rejoinder, a distant rattle and throbbing caught her attention. 'What's that?' She cocked her ear towards the noise. 'I'm sure I can hear something. Like a motor.'

Spinning around, Mitch stood in silence, obviously straining his ears to listen. 'You're right. It's coming from behind us.'

'But there's no road there!' Grace frowned and peered back across the dusty plain they'd just crossed. What on earth could be coming from that direction? A station owner in a four-wheel drive?

In the distance, a dark blob was beginning to take shape. 'Oh, my goodness,' she breathed. The emerging form was nothing like what she expected. Instead of a battered but friendly cattleman's truck, a squat, sinister-looking, camouflaged vehicle rumbled towards them. 'Who on earth could *they* be?' she croaked.

She edged closer to Mitch. 'They've got guns. Have— have we been invaded or something?'

Mitch frowned, pulled a doubtful face and shook his head. 'They have two machine guns mounted on the cabin,' he commented as he squinted at them, 'but they don't seem to be ready for action.' He flashed her a tight smile, before screwing up his eyes to watch the approaching vehicle.

'But there's another gun!' she insisted, her voice sharp with fear. 'See the fellow riding on the bonnet—' She broke off on a note of sheer panic.

Mitch threw a comforting arm around her shaking shoulders. 'You've been watching too many movies, Grace.'

'Movies, Mr Director, can be very educational.'

Mitch granted her half a smile and he gave her shoulder a reassuring squeeze. 'I'll admit that fellow does have some kind of automatic weapon, but look, he's just got it slung over his shoulder. I don't think he intends to start shooting at us.'

But Grace wouldn't be mollified. How could Mitch stay so calm? For heaven's sake, strange soldiers wouldn't be travelling in this remote, northern part of the country unless something had gone seriously wrong.

'Mitch,' she whispered. 'They look so threatening. Could Australia have been invaded while we've been lost? We should have stayed at the rock pool.'

The roar of the vehicle grew louder as it neared them. Grace realised she was clutching Mitch's arm with the desperation of a victim of the *Titanic*. She was sure she was about to die. She would be shot or, at the very least, dragged away and raped before being murdered.

'I'm sure they're not aggressive,' Mitch muttered.

'Then why aren't you waving or acting friendly?'

'For heaven's sake, woman. Just let me deal with this.'

'Sure,' she fumed, with an impatient roll of her eyes skywards. Mitch was back in fearless leader mode. But perhaps that was just as well, she conceded as she cowered behind him and held her breath while the vehicle slowed to a halt.

Silently, the men scrambled out of the cabin and, with the menacing agility of a panther, the figure on the bonnet leaped to the ground.

Mitch was frowning.

Grace's heart thudded a deafening tattoo. Every one of these creatures was armed and their faces were smudged with green and black paint.

Out of the corner of her eye, she saw Mitch's puzzled expression melt slowly. And then she realised these men were all grinning broadly. An alert-looking fellow stepped forward and extended his hand to Mitch. 'Dr Livingstone, I presume?' he drawled with a distinctly Australian accent.

Mitch actually laughed as he shook the young man's

hand heartily. 'G'day. Good to see you. Surely the Australian Army hasn't sent you looking for us?'

'Lieutenant Ripley,' the other fellow introduced himself, returning Mitch's handshake. 'We're a reconnaissance squad based in Townsville and we're up here on remote area exercises.' He nodded his head towards the fellow who'd been riding the bonnet. 'This is Freddie Day. He's our company's top tracker. We found a burnt-out vehicle early this morning—'

'That was ours,' Mitch interrupted.

'We know,' grinned Ripley. 'I decided it presented us with a pretty good challenge to test our squad's tracking abilities under real conditions. So here we are. Freddie's been following your tracks since then.'

'I'll be blowed; that's pretty quick work.' Mitch grinned back at them.

Grace sidled forward to take a closer look at their rescuers. Some were wearing floppy bush hats and two had heads covered by green bandannas that made them look like buccaneers, but now that she knew who they were she realised that none of them looked sinister.

Mitch completed the introductions. 'I'm Mitch Wentworth and this is Grace Robbins, my—' He flashed her a swift, secretive, almost possessive look that made her toes curl. 'Grace is my assistant. We left Townsville at the weekend and were checking out locations for Tropicana Films when we ran into trouble with the vehicle.'

'You did the right thing heading towards the coast,' Ripley said. 'That rock pool you found is the only water in about a fifty-kilometre radius of here.'

Mitch thumped Grace's shoulder and winked at her. 'That was Grace's bright idea. I wanted to stay with the vehicle.'

'Well done, ma'am. You saved your lives,' commented

the man called Freddie Day. 'This was one of the few situations where staying with the vehicle would have been the wrong decision.' His face creased into a lazy, knowing smile and his eyes focused on Mitch. 'You had a cosy little campsite back at the rock pool.'

Grace had the awful feeling that this expert tracker, who had followed their trail so easily through such rugged terrain, would have taken one look at the imprint of their bodies where she and Mitch had slept and known exactly how *cosy* they had been.

Was she imagining it, or were all the soldiers exchanging covert glances and doing their best to hide knowing smirks?

Lieutenant Ripley held out a satellite phone to Mitch. 'Would you like to advise anyone of your whereabouts?'

'Yes, sure. Thanks, mate.' Mitch took the phone and strode some distance away to make his call. Grace watched him, noting his intense concentration as he spoke, the way he clutched the phone with one hand while gesticulating and explaining with the other, and she sensed him metamorphosing before her.

Turning back into her boss.

As one phone call was completed, he made another. And another. The soldiers, obviously uneasy about making polite conversation with her, chatted amongst themselves until Mitch was finished.

'We can take you both back to our base camp and then chopper you back to Townsville, if you like,' Ripley offered as Mitch returned.

'Wonderful.' Mitch held his hand out to Grace to help her up into the awkwardly high vehicle and she hesitated, staring at his sunburnt, outstretched hand.

They were going back.

Just like that. One minute they were about to make love

in the outback in the shade of a clump of gum trees and the next they were heading back to Townsville.

To the office.

To their other world of phone calls and faxes, computer printouts and inter-office memos, meetings and briefings...

Business! Other people. Other women.

She looked up at Mitch as she gave him her hand and his dark eyes probed her with a confusing intensity. In a worried daze, she climbed into the troop carrier and took the seat provided, her mind refusing to let go of an over-whelming sense of loss. She was being rescued, for heaven's sake. Why on earth did she feel so morbid?

She knew Mitch would tell her she was being silly, but she was quite, quite certain that it wasn't just the outback she was leaving. She was leaving behind the wonderful, astonishing thing that had happened to her and Mitch while they were lost.

Mitch swung into the seat beside her, and Lieutenant Ripley placed himself opposite. Two more men climbed in while the other soldiers seemed content to hang onto the outside. And, even before the vehicle roared forward once more, Mitch and Ripley began chatting like old friends.

While the men discussed the unit's recent involvement with the United Nations in Africa, Cambodia and Timor, Grace watched silently. Mitch seemed very at home. He was surprisingly knowledgeable about international affairs. She watched his relaxed smile and the genuine interest with which he listened to the other men. It was as if he'd known these strangers for years. It must be a blokey thing, she decided with a sigh.

He almost completely ignored her. Already it was hard to believe she had spent the past two days doing little else but make love with him. Why, just this morning, she had lain by the rock pool in his arms and he had kissed and caressed her and had murmured her name over and over as if he had been trying to fuse her identity with his. Several times she'd been on the brink of telling him how much his lovemaking meant to her.

How much *he* meant to her.

At the rock pool, she had *almost* allowed herself to think about *love*. Now, as they rattled across the stubbled plains, she thanked heavens that she hadn't said anything foolish about her feelings.

By the time they reached the base camp, Mitch was negotiating to use the army as extras and as advisors in the survival and battle scenes of *New Tomorrow*.

He flashed her an excited grin as he turned to her. 'Isn't this fantastic, Grace? Just what we need.'

'Great,' she agreed, with a forced smile. And, of course, it was. She wanted the very best for *New Tomorrow*, too. Until two days ago, the success of the company, and this film in particular, had been the central focus of her life.

For a brief moment in time, Mitch had caused a huge shift in her focus. But it was clear that, now she was returning to the real world, she would have to readjust her sights. In a few short hours they would be back in Townsville and she would be Ms Robbins, director's assistant.

And Mitch would be simply her boss.

Three hours later, the Black Hawk helicopter chugged and dipped in its descent to the helipad at Townsville's Lavarack Barracks, before finally settling on the ground. A huge metal door slid open, and Mitch stood, stretched and smiled down at Grace. She permitted herself the luxury of basking in that smile and allowed her gaze to linger for a moment on his delicious mouth and sexy brown eyes.

He placed a hand at her elbow. 'Ready to go?' he asked.

'Sure.' She swallowed back the painful lump in her throat as she allowed him to help her to her feet, and followed him out of the helicopter and down the short ladder. And she tried to shake off the heavy weight of her depression. These stinging eyes and the choky feeling in her throat were quite uncalled for. Ridiculous. She blinked and took in a deep breath.

Above them, the rotor blades stopped circling, and a predictable cluster of men in military fatigues stepped forward to greet them.

It was only as Grace's dusty walking boots hit the tarmac that she saw the woman. The woman with a heart-shaped face and eyes bigger than the Ross River Dam. The petite platinum-blonde in a hot-pink mini skirt and jacket with sheer black stockings and sinfully high heeled shoes.

'Da-ar-arling.' Her voice and her clothes smacked of Hollywood as she tottered towards Mitch and launched herself into his arms. 'Are you okay, you poor, dear baby?'

# CHAPTER NINE

MITCH looked momentarily ambushed. 'Candy! I didn'—' His words were cut off as the woman rose onto tiptoes and smacked a noisy kiss on his mouth.

Grace's teeth clenched.

Candy lowered her heels to the ground and moaned, 'Where have you *been*, Mitch?'

He shook his head as he smiled back at her. 'I should have realised you'd be part of the welcoming party, when I heard you were in town.'

'You bad boy. Of course I had to come rushing straight out here to check for myself that you're okay.' She ran a possessive hand down his cheek and a heavy gold charm bracelet glinted in the sun. 'I've been so worried about you.'

Mitch frowned. 'But no one knew we were in any kind of trouble till I telephoned this morning.'

'Yes. But since *then*, baby. I've been going through all sorts of agony.' Her painted lips pouted.

Turning inside the tight circle of Candy's embrace, Mitch sent a quick smile Grace's way. 'We're well and quite fit, aren't we, Grace?'

'As a fiddle,' she agreed, her tone one hundred per cent acid.

Candy took a step back from Mitch, but left one arm draped around his waist. Her round blue eyes narrowed as they confronted Grace.

And Grace was suddenly acutely conscious of her bedraggled appearance. She didn't need to see her reflection

116

in any mirror. She could just imagine how she looked, with stringy, unbrushed hair, stained and considerably rumpled clothes and her face burnt by the sun.

The waiting military people stepped forward, introduced themselves, and Mitch thanked them for their help. During the exchange, Candy seemed to continue her study of Grace. She forced a smile that, in Grace's opinion, seemed as artificial as her hair colour.

'Mitch, baby, you must introduce me to your little secretary.'

*Secretary!* Silent rage bristled in her throat. Her work involved much more than secretarial duties, and she suspected Candy knew it.

She might have seethed and fumed some more if Mitch hadn't stepped away from Candy and reached for Grace's hand, drawing her closer.

'Candy, let me introduce the most brilliant assistant any director could ask for, Grace Robbins.'

The two women exchanged handshakes. Candy's hand was cool and limp and Grace decided that her thick black eyelashes were also fake.

'Grace,' Mitch continued, 'this is Candy Sorbell, the woman I most have to impress.'

'Oh?' Grace found it so hard to keep the coolness out of her voice.

'Oh, yes. She's the infamous tight-fisted finance executive from High Sierra Studios in L.A.'

'High Sierra?' Grace echoed. Film companies didn't come much bigger.

'Now, Mitch.' Candy pouted. 'I'm only tight-fisted if I'm not treated right.'

Mitch's chuckle was thin. Grace shivered.

'But let's not worry about that now,' Candy said, shaking her fist so the heavy charm bracelet jangled. 'You've been through a ghastly ordeal, you poor man, and you should be home in your hotel. I know exactly what you need. A nice hot bath, a decent meal and an early night. You should be tucked up in bed by—'

'Mitch,' Grace broke in quietly. 'Do you still have that phone? I'd like to organise a taxi.'

Mitch frowned. 'For you, Grace? There's no need. I'm sure Candy would be happy to give you a—'

'Oh, of course, we can do that for you, sweetie,' interrupted Candy with an enthusiastic grin that would have done a used-car salesman proud. She grabbed a mobile phone from her handbag. 'Here you are. Help yourself. That's very thoughtful of you to take a taxi home so I can hurry your poor boss straight off to his hotel.'

'Thanks,' muttered Grace.

'No,' interrupted Mitch sternly. 'We're not going to just leave Grace to make her own way home.'

Candy's eyebrows rose.

One of the army officers stepped forward and cleared his throat deferentially. 'We'd be only too happy to provide transport for Miss Robbins,' he said.

'Thank you so much.' Grace sent the man a warm smile, knowing that she couldn't take much more of Candy. The woman produced more gushing than the spas at Hot Springs. She turned to Mitch and hoped her voice sounded more steady than she felt. 'Please, go back to your hotel and get some—rest. I'll be absolutely fine.'

'I'm absolutely fine,' Grace repeated much later when an agitated Maria phoned her.

'You're sure you're okay? Not suffering from—um—exposure?'

Grace suppressed a sigh. Her exposed emotions had taken quite a battering, but she presumed Maria was referring to physical exposure to the elements in the harsh out-back. 'We were lucky the tropical winters are so mild,' she explained. 'The middle of the day was pretty hot, but on the whole I haven't had any problems. And now I've had a lovely bath—the longest, hottest, sudsiest soak of my life. I'm shampooed and moisturised. I've put aloe vera on my sunburn, and I'm stretched out on the sofa with a lovely glass of chilled wine.' Grace took a deep swig of the wine. 'I feel great,' she lied.

'Okay, you've convinced me.' Maria laughed. 'I'm so relieved.'

There was a short silence. And Grace, feeling the kind of physical relaxation that comes from a hot bath, clean hair and weary muscles, snuggled lower on the sofa and took another sip of wine.

'So, come on, kiddo,' urged Maria. 'Spill the beans. Tell Aunt Maria all about it.'

Some of Grace's relaxation began to slip away. 'I've already told you everything about the accident and finding the rock pool. And then the army...'

'Yeah. But I want to know about the serious stuff.'

'Being lost had its serious moments.' She was hedging, aware that Maria had a nose for scandal as finely tuned as any member of the paparazzi's.

'Grace, are you stringing me along? You spent three days alone in the wilderness with the studliest of all studs. Come on,' she urged, her voice sounding as if she was going through some kind of endurance test. 'Give me just a hint.'

'Maria, there's nothing to hint about. We survived. We found water, and crayfish to eat.'

A swear word blasted from the other end of the line. 'Listen to me, Grace Robbins. If you haven't allowed your-self to experience the full force of Mitch Wentworth's—

er—attention, you've—you've committed a crime agains
the feminine gender.'

'For crying out loud!'

'You got together with Mitch, didn't you? I can tell. H
hit on you, Grace, and you succumbed.'

Grace felt cold wine trickling beneath the gaping neck
line of her bathrobe and realised she was shaking. She se
the wineglass on the floor beside her. *He hit on you an*
*you succumbed.* Maria had smacked the bull's eye with he
first shot. But how terribly basic and ordinary she made i
sound!

And predictable. She'd fallen for Mitch just as she ha
feared she would. Mitch had only to…

Guiltily, Grace remembered that the situation was eve
worse than Maria had suggested. Mitch hadn't seduced her
*He hadn't lifted a finger!*

*She* had begged *him* to kiss her! And, of course, she ha
known exactly what would follow.

'I see.' Maria was purring into the phone. 'My dear girl
your silence is bellowing. All I can say is, good on you
And I'm emerald with envy.'

'No, Maria. You've got it wrong—'

There was a firm rat-a-tat on her door. 'Look, I have t
go. There's someone at the door,' she added with relief.

'Sure there is,' grumbled Maria. 'And I came down i
the last shower. Grace, you don't—'

Grace jumped to her feet and headed across the room
taking the cordless phone with her and frowning as Mari
launched into another tirade. She swung the door open.

Mitch.

He stood there, clean and freshly shaven, in a whit
T-shirt that made his tan look darker than ever, smiling hi
lazy, heart-lurching smile, with his hands shoved into th

pockets of his jeans. Questions about a certain blonde with a very sweet name flashed into Grace's head.

And out again.

'We have matters to discuss,' he said. His hands came out of his pockets and he drew her towards him, planting a warm, hungry kiss on her mouth.

The phone slipped to the floor and landed on Grace's doormat with a soft thud.

*'Grace, are you there?'*

Dimly, she was aware of Maria's frantic voice. But Mitch's mouth was demanding her attention—her undivided attention. She might have asked for that first kiss by the campfire, but now his kiss made all kinds of intimate requests. There was no doubting the urgent pleading of that tongue, seeking out hers, or that hard male body pressing itself firmly against her.

'Missed me?' he murmured against her ear.

'Oh, yes.' His skin smelled clean and just a little spicy, and it was warm and sensuous beneath her lips.

'You know, you have the sexiest mouth.' He nibbled at her full lower lip.

*'Is that Mitch? Is he there with you now?'* Maria's screech crackled at their feet.

'What the—?' Mitch looked just a little startled.

'Shh,' Grace warned, with a finger to her lips. She pointed to the phone on the mat and stooped to pick it up.

'Sorry, Maria,' she said into the receiver. 'My neighbour dropped in. She's—she's been looking after my goldfish. I had to—' Mitch nuzzled her neck, making it very difficult to keep the tremble out of her voice. 'When she handed over the tank, I dropped the phone.'

'Your neighbour? But I thought your neighbour was an old lady.'

Through the thin green silk of her robe, Mitch's hands

traced Grace's backbone. They reached her bottom. For more reasons than one, sweat filmed her body. 'Ah, that's right, Maria. Mrs Nye lives next door. She's a real sweetie.'

'But I was sure I heard a man's voice. Grace, are you okay? You're kind of panting into the phone.'

The phone was snatched from Grace's hand. A strong masculine finger depressed a button.

And that was the end of Maria.

Grace stared at the phone as Mitch tossed it onto a large floor cushion. 'That was Maria Cavalero,' she cried. 'She will never forgive me for cutting her off. And the whole office will be buzzing with scandal tomorrow.'

He frowned. 'Why didn't you turn the darned phone off earlier?'

'You caught me by surprise.'

Mitch grinned slyly. 'I guess I did.'

'I wasn't expecting you, and I certainly didn't know you were going to start kissing me before you got through my front door.'

Lowering himself onto the sofa, he pulled Grace down to his lap. 'Just because we're back in civilisation doesn't mean we have to be civilised.'

'You're sure?' She smiled into his mouth as he nuzzled it against hers.

There was no answer. Just that mind-numbing, persuasive pressure of his mouth teasing hers. His hands nudging the silky robe from her shoulders. His breath catching as he found the soft curve of her breast. And his voice groaning her name.

'You'll have to help me make up some kind of convincing story to keep Maria quiet,' she murmured dreamily as wave upon dizzying wave of pleasure spread through her.

Mitch tensed in her arms. His head lifted, and he stared ahead bleakly. 'Cavalero's a motormouth?' he queried.

Startled by his abrupt mood change, Grace sat rather self-consciously on his lap. 'She has been known to gossip, but I'm sure Maria can be discreet,' she quickly amended, not wanting to get her friend into hot water. 'It's just that she loves romance. The faintest hint and she's—'

'Romance?' interrupted Mitch, frowning at her once more.

Grace slid from his lap to sit beside him on the sofa. Nervously she tucked stray strands of hair behind her ear. She was suddenly frightened by the wary darkness in his expression. 'I don't mean—I—I mean I'm not talking about *romantic* happy-ever-after romance. It's just that she's very into—you know—girl-guy stuff…hormonal activity,' she mumbled, embarrassed.

For a brief moment, Mitch's mouth twitched with amusement, but a more serious expression quickly replaced the bare glimmer of a smile. 'Actually, I came here tonight to sort out this employer-employee situation,' he said with a sigh.

'I see,' Grace said softly.

'Then somehow I got sidetracked,' he added with a wry grimace.

'You seem to make a habit of leaving the track, Mr Wentworth.' She sat very stiffly, quite certain that Mitch was going to explain, just as Roger had three years earlier, that their little affair, interlude, or whatever he might want to call it, was going to get in the way of business.

Wearily, Mitch leant his head back against the sofa, and the light from the nearby table-lamp played across his face. For the first time since he'd arrived, Grace saw the deep lines of exhaustion around his eyes and at the sides of his mouth.

His forehead wrinkled, creasing the lines more deeply. 'I like to think I'm a man who learns from his mistakes.

Professionally, I'm in a vulnerable position at the moment—putting all my eggs in one basket. I can't afford foolish slips.'

*Foolish slips?*

*She was a foolish slip?*

How could she prevent herself from weeping? If only she had trusted her initial instincts about her boss. Instead, she'd been swept away by his looks and his charm and she'd very nearly lost her heart in the process.

'You don't have to spell out how you want me to behave in the office,' she said carefully, her voice only just steady. 'I understand how complicated and inappropriate it would be if anyone suspected we had…been…been *involved.*'

He nodded, and Grace bit down hard on her lip. When he stared at her lip protruding from her clenched teeth, she had to turn away.

She had certainly been very, very naive. On the other hand, Mitch had simply stayed true to type. For a brief moment in the bush, the international playboy had dallied with a new playmate. She'd been the only available female at the time and, to make matters ten times worse, she'd thrown herself at him. It was as predictable as the changing of the seasons that he would have seized the opportunity to hone his sporting skills some more.

Feeling like a silly, witless Mitch Wentworth groupie, Grace inched away from him. He must never suspect that his lovemaking had been more wonderful than anything she'd ever known. And he must certainly never know that she had fancied herself in love with him. A man like Mitch didn't care for women who allowed their emotions to become entangled with their hormones.

Mitch switched his gaze to stare at her hand-woven rug as he spoke. 'This would all be so much easier if you weren't working for me. Office affairs are so darned inconvenient.'

*Inconvenient?* First she was a foolish slip, and now she was an inconvenience.

In a matter of seconds, Grace's swelling sense of misery dissolved and honest-to-goodness anger—her original feeling for this man—swiftly took its place. 'You've got a nerve,' she said. 'It would be a jolly sight more convenient for me if *you* weren't my *boss!*'

She jumped to her feet and crossed her arms belligerently over her chest. Her robe was gaping. Taking a moment to tug the neckline together, she re-crossed her arms. 'But I have no plans to go hunting for another job, *Mr* Wentworth.'

With a softly muttered curse, Mitch rose from the sofa, and Grace stepped back as his height unfurled before her. 'I'm not asking you to resign, Grace. I'm just acknowledging that we have a—potentially contentious situation at the office.'

'And you think rushing around to my flat tonight and kissing me in full public view on my front doorstep is the best way to solve it?'

Mitch's eyes widened and he scratched his head.

*No,* Grace tried to convince herself, *he does not look like a really cute little boy with a puzzle to solve.*

'I guess I hadn't considered that risk factor. But you said yourself that Maria Cavalero could cause problems.'

'And you said my working for you was a problem.'

'I was talking in general terms—the whole boss and employee scenario.'

Tapping her bare foot against the floor, Grace willed herself to stay calm and logical and to forget about how good it felt to be wrapped in his arms. She was fighting for her job now. 'If you are suggesting that my employment is a risk factor, you can think again. I love my work. It means everything to me.' She took a deep, rallying breath before she issued her ultimatum. 'I can manage quite nicely without your kisses, Mitch, but I can't give up my position at Tropicana Films.'

His eyes widened. For a second, Grace thought she saw a flicker of admiration, but she was too hurt and angry to stop and consider his reaction to her outburst.

'And I'd like you to leave now,' she added. 'We don't want anyone to think you'd lingered too long at my flat tonight.'

'Hold it, Grace. I think you're getting irrational about this. Don't get heated. I just wanted to—'

'Clear the air?' she supplied through gritted teeth as she sailed past him in the direction of her door. 'Consider the air clear, Mr Wentworth. And the slate's clean, too. No problem. All obstacles have been swept away. And you can make a fresh start in the morning with no nasty little innuendoes from me. I'll go back to work tomorrow as your assistant and—and—' she faltered for a moment '—I'll leave anything else to Candy Sorbell.'

'Candy? How does she come into this?'

Grace shook her head very slowly and sighed. 'Ask her. I'm sure she'll be only too happy to explain, and if you are still having difficulty understanding she can provide very helpful practical demonstrations.'

'Grace, for Pete's sake, I didn't come here to get you mad at me again.'

'I'm sure you didn't. That's why you were going to suggest I leave the company.' Choking down her fury, Grace flung her door open and with a dramatic gesture pointed the way down her front path.

Mitch stepped towards her. 'Grace, we can work something out.' He lifted a hand to her cheek.

But she flicked her face sideways so that no connection was made. 'I have the perfect solution,' she told him. 'If you're uncomfortable about our working relationship, why don't you go find yourself another film company to take over? Give Tropicana back to poor George Hervey. He didn't deserve to have the company he'd struggled to build up snatched away from him like *that*!' Her last words were accompanied by an angry snap of her fingers.

By the time she finished, she could see that Mitch was angry, too. His eyes were hard and glassy and his lips were compressed into a thin, pale line. His voice, when he spoke, was very low. 'If that's where you're coming from, then I'd be wasting my time trying to discuss any other point of view with you.'

Grace asked herself why his sudden acquiescence left her feeling as if she'd lost something. Surely this was a moment of victory?

Mitch dipped his head briefly in her direction and stepped past her out of the flat. 'I don't think there is anything helpful that can be added to this conversation. Goodnight.'

'Goodnight,' she whispered as he disappeared into the black of night. For a few moments longer, she could hear his footsteps ringing out his departure on the concrete driveway.

Then she shut her door and burst into tears.

# CHAPTER TEN

MITCH lifted his wineglass to the light so he could examine the full-bodied red he'd ordered. It looked superb and, two sips later, he knew he'd made a wise choice. The Hunter Valley wine was dry and mellow—very good indeed.

Life was getting better by the minute.

Ever since Grace had accepted his invitation to dinner a short time earlier, he'd felt buoyed by a renewed sense of optimism. After last night, it was important to get this matter with her sorted out properly. The way things had ended up was totally unsatisfactory and he'd been rattled more than he cared to admit by her sudden, angry outburst.

But yesterday they'd been tired, their emotions overwrought on account of their ordeal.

They couldn't remain prickly and avoiding each other. It was an untenable working situation.

Tonight they could talk things over quietly and rationally.

Another sip of wine and Mitch congratulated himself on choosing the large and popular restaurant attached to the hotel where he was staying. To anyone inclined to speculate, it would look totally above board—a business meeting. He'd brought a pile of business papers and placed them on the table in front of him, to make that point clear.

But he was actually planning a very different discussion. He and Grace had some important bridges to build.

A jangle of jewellery and a cloud of exotic perfume interrupted his pleasant musings.

'Mitch! A working dinner and, darling, dining alone? We

can't have that.' Candy Sorbell, in something orange, skin-tight and probably very expensive, dropped into the chair opposite him, apparently seeing no significance in the fact that his table was set for two.

'Good evening, Candy.' Mitch smiled politely, if not warmly.

'What are you drinking?' she asked loudly like a bright, annoying parrot.

He indicated the excellent wine.

'Nah.' Candy pulled a face. 'I need something that packs a punch.'

With a barely suppressed sigh, Mitch beckoned a waiter, and while the young man made his way to their table Candy prattled on. 'I decided to take a rain check on that concert, Mitch. I know you Australians have culture; you don't have to ram it down my throat.'

Mitch inclined his head with another polite smile. 'You're probably very tired.'

She leaned forward, offering him a generous view of her tanned cleavage before fixing him with her shrewd blue gaze. 'I've been expending a lot of energy trying to save your seat, Mitch. I talked to Joe again today. It was 6 a.m. in L.A. and he wasn't too happy, but it was the only time I could be sure of catching him. I was trying to get him to ease off on you for a few more days. Oh, an extra-dry martini, thanks, honey,' she added with a flutter of her eye-lashes for the waiter. Then her expression hardened as she hissed at Mitch, 'I sure hope they know how to make a decent martini here.'

But Mitch didn't reply. He could see Grace standing in the restaurant's entrance, frowning as she looked in his direction.

He waved and tried to swallow away the sudden constriction in his throat. Grace was wearing a simple black and white striped dress that skimmed softly over her body, hinting at the perfection underneath. He sent her a smile.

Dimly, he heard Candy's voice. 'That's your little secretary, isn't it? What's she doing here?'

'She's joining me for dinner,' he muttered tersely out of the corner of his mouth.

'Oh, how quaint,' Candy murmured. 'It would be useful for me to get to know some more of your staff.'

The calculated, steely note in her voice sounded to Mitch like a definite warning.

Grace was grateful that the restaurant's receptionist was busy with a customer. She needed a moment to gather her wits and to figure out how it would look if she turned and walked straight back out of the hotel. The sight of Candy Sorbell, chatting so intimately with Mitch, ruined her appetite. And it prompted her to wonder what had happened to her brains in the past few days. Had she become so moronic that she'd imagined Mitch wanted to dine alone with her?

After last night?

Ever since he'd left her flat, she'd been unbearably miserable, and all day she'd known that she really needed to talk to him again. When his invitation had appeared amidst her e-mail messages, she'd mulled it over for some time. Eventually, she'd decided it was important to get things absolutely straight.

Glancing at his table again, she sighed. There'd be no straight talking here in this cosy little threesome. She reached into her purse for her car keys. It would be better if she left now. Candy wouldn't care. And Mitch...

Mitch, wearing a navy sports jacket and a snowy white shirt, was rising to his feet, his eyes fixed fiercely on her.

Grace's heart melted at the intensity of his expression and her hesitation dissolved. The keys slid back into her purse.

He took a step towards her and, as if hypnotised by his dark gaze, she began to make her way across the room, weaving between the tables of chatting diners.

Halfway there, too late to turn back, she saw Candy reach out a suntanned, lean arm to grab Mitch's elbow. His attention caught, she was obviously urging him back into his seat and engaging him with animated conversation.

As she reached them, Grace's simmering emotions bubbled to quick anger.

Especially when Candy blithely ignored her and kept talking to Mitch as she waved a glass in one hand and rattled her bracelet. Mitch was giving strange sideways jerks of his head as he tried to break into the conversation and greet Grace.

'I keep telling Joe that anything you are excited about has to be a winner,' Candy was saying loudly. As she spoke, she stroked his arm, possessively, suggestively. 'I've worked with you before, darling, so I know just what you have to offer.'

Grace hovered.

Candy paused for breath and Mitch leapt to his feet. 'Grace, thanks for coming.' He held out his hand to take hers rather formally. 'Now,' he said solicitously, 'you take my chair and I'll grab a waiter to get us another and set an extra place.'

When these little formalities were attended to and the three sat facing each other, Mitch shot her a look loaded with meaning. 'Candy has rearranged her evening so that she's able to join us.'

'How nice.' Grace forced a smile and nodded to Candy. She always hated those awkward silences that sometimes followed introductions. But for the life of her she couldn't think of anything else to say. *Now what?*

And she was answered more quickly than she expected. 'This is just great to have you here,' over-enthused Candy. 'Mitch tells me you're such an efficient secretary. Did you bring a notebook and pencil? There might be a few points we raise tonight that Mitch will want jotted down.'

At what temperature did blood boil? Grace could hardly conceal her indignation. Her eyes shot sideways to Mitch and she was a little mollified by the shock and embarrassment she read in his expression.

'I doubt that will be necessary, Candy,' he responded quickly. 'Grace, let me pour you some of this delightful wine.'

But Grace's green eyes were not simply a genetic accident. A challenge had been laid and her chin lifted as she decided to play Candy's game. She always carried a small notepad and pen in her handbag and she retrieved them now, flipped the pad open to a clean page and sat with the pen poised. Baring her teeth at Candy, she said sweetly, 'Go ahead, Ms Sorbell. I'm all ready to take notes.'

'Ah, sure.' Candy looked just a little taken aback, but after a hefty swig of her martini she continued. 'That's good, thank you, dear. Now, Mitch. Where were we?'

'We were about to order dinner and we are going to leave business aside for a while,' Mitch said firmly. He picked up his own menu and began to study it assiduously.

With one eyebrow raised in a fretful arc, Candy shrugged unhappily and hastily scanned her menu. 'I'll just have a Caesar salad,' she muttered, and swung one foot impatiently while the others took their time choosing their meals.

As soon as the orders were placed, Mitch spoke, throwing a question casually onto the table and not aiming it at anyone in particular. 'I hear Magnetic Island is very pleasant and it's only a short ferry ride away from Townsville. Perhaps we should explore it on the weekend?'

'Haven't you two done enough exploring in the outdoors for this week?' snapped Candy. Her eyes slid to Grace. 'Poor Grace's nose couldn't take any more sun.'

Grace smiled thinly.

'Really, Mitch,' Candy hurried on. 'All this sightseeing, concerts, the theatre. I'm not here on holiday. We need to focus on business.' She leaned forward again, and Grace couldn't help wondering if the impressive cleavage was as fake as the hair colour and the eyelashes. 'And the message I bring from my company to you—'

'Just a minute.' Grace made a flurried display of taking up her notebook and pencil.

Mitch frowned and Candy stared at her coldly, but continued. 'This *New Tomorrow* project of yours is only going to work if you get High Sierra's backing. You really must settle the deal over a drink, tonight. Now.'

'I very much doubt that's possible,' Mitch replied smoothly.

Grace regarded the two of them. What on earth was she doing here? This was power play, and way out of her territory. Perhaps this dinner was a deliberate ploy of Mitch's to put her in her place? She looked at the pile of papers beside him.

*How ridiculous that I've imagined an intimate dinner alone with him, holding hands across the table, drinking in his sexy smile. Making up…*

Her pencil dug sharp, angry strokes onto the page.

Candy was getting heated. 'Are you playing games with me, Mitch? Look, if you come to the party, Joe's agreed. The money is yours, as long as you accept our terms. All we're asking is fifty-one per cent and exclusive world distribution rights.'

'Fifty-one per cent…' Grace parroted as she jotted down the figures. Candy glared at her, and Grace frowned at the page and stuck out her tongue as if concentrating on the task of note-taking were very difficult.

Mitch sighed in obvious irritation. 'You know I'm only prepared to offer twenty per cent. And then there are all your *other* conditions.' He shot an anxious glance towards Grace. 'They're too steep, Candy.'

Grace, feeling totally furious and very out of place, made some more noisy scribbles on the page. 'Would you like me to list those conditions?'

An angry red tinge crept along Mitch's cheekbones. He scowled at her. 'Grace, what on earth do you think you're doing? Don't be stupid.'

She blinked at him and then, fuming, rose to her feet, her anger giving the movement a surprising degree of majesty. 'On this occasion, I'm doing very little,' she replied icily.

Of all the arrogant men! There was only so much she could take. Not so long ago, Henry had called her stupid. And now Mitch. She admitted to many faults, but stupidity was not one of them.

As she stood there, her gaze darting from one to the other, Mitch's startled expression was too unsettling, so she addressed Candy. 'I'm sorry to leave you like this, but my understanding was that this evening was purely social.' Hardly believing her own actions, she tossed the notebook and pen onto the table in front of Candy. 'I'll leave these for you in case you *really do need* to make notes.'

With an abrupt about-turn, she hurried away, almost colliding with the waiter bringing their meals. Out of habit, she experienced a momentary pang of guilt about wasting the food she'd ordered. But then, she reminded herself, the people she was abandoning were not like her frugal parents. They handled multi-million-dollar deals without turning a hair and, at a pinch, they could manage to foot the bill for one small serving of satay beef with a green salad.

Mitch called her name, but she didn't look back. She dodged her way through the tables as annoying tears welled in her eyes and, by the time she reached the marbled expanse of the hotel foyer, her chin was trembling.

Behind her, there were hurried footsteps, but again she refused to turn around. Under no circumstances would she be coerced back to that table.

She sniffed and tossed her head defiantly high and sailed down the smooth, wide hotel steps, like Cinderella rushing from the ball. If Mitch had followed her, she didn't want to know about it. She continued on down the softly lit path, as it swept in a long curve past tropical palms and clumps of spider lilies, to the car park.

It was only as she reached her car that she realised there were no more footsteps. She looked behind her. No one was following.

And suddenly she was disappointed. An embarrassing sob erupted. *What had she been expecting? A fairy-tale reunion with Mitch under the tropical stars?*

Dream on.

Mitch was focused on money and movies. Power and fame. Not love.

Never love.

She wrenched her car door open, slumped into the driver's seat and slammed the door closed again. Never had she felt more alone and vulnerable. Up here in North Queensland, she was away from family and old friends and she'd fallen uselessly in love with her boss.

Her hands gripped the steering wheel and she rested her

head against them. Her face felt hot and wet. Heavens above, what had happened to her? Until recently, she'd always stayed calm in the face of difficulty. She'd prided herself on her problem-solving ability and, at the very least, she'd thought she was mature enough to adjust to changing circumstances.

But the most recent major change in her working life—a new boss—had sent her to pieces. An emotional heap. She rubbed her eyes with clenched knuckles. Perhaps she would have to think about another job.

There was a sharp crack of shoes on the gravel outside. Startled, she peered into the darkness through tear-blurred eyes. Her door opened.

'Grace, what do you think you're playing at?' A furious Mitch bent down to glare at her.

No Prince Charming searching for his lost love. Just a very angry boss. Grace gulped back another sob and prayed that, in the dark, he couldn't see her tear-streaked face.

'What is it with you women?'

*Wasn't he supposed to be an expert with women?* 'I'm not *playing* at anything,' she cried. 'But I can't vouch for Candy Sorbell's motives.'

Mitch shook his head. 'Leave Candy out of this for the moment.'

'With pleasure.' *Whoosh.* She let out her breath. 'I thought, when you invited me to dinner, that you wanted to talk to me.'

Instead of replying, he sighed and leaned his back against the side of her car. He stared at the night sky. Grace waited for him to speak. She could hear, in the nearby marina, a motor boat's engine begin to chug and she saw the way the sea breeze lifted Mitch's dark hair.

It wasn't fair that, in the moonlight, he still looked like

every woman's dream come true. How could a man be so confusingly arrogant and so dreamy at the same time?

'Of course I want to talk to you privately,' he said at last.

'Then what is Candy doing at our table? Why didn't you get rid of her?'

He shoved his hands deep into the pockets of his trousers. 'It's not that easy. I can't just send her packing.'

'You can't or you don't want to?' Grace's hands gripped the steering wheel once more.

'I can't and I'm not going to,' Mitch told her quietly. He turned and there was no smile, only a brooding frown.

Her bitter laugh sounded distinctly catty, but she couldn't help it. 'Are you and Candy Sorbell going to be the small print in the contract with High Sierra?'

'Now you're going too far.' His palm thumped into the side of the car. 'How did you dream up that crazy idea?'

Again, Grace laughed, but it trailed off into an uncertain little cough as she realised that she had steered this conversation into dangerous waters. Without even trying, she was slap bang in the middle of another argument with Mitch. And the tide of their angry feelings was so strong that she couldn't turn back. She didn't even have time to think out a way to direct herself onto safe ground.

Mitch lowered his head to speak softly through the open doorway. His voice was deep and persuasive. 'Come back and sweat it out for just a little longer, Grace. I'll try to get rid of Candy later.'

Incredulous, she stared at him, trying to understand. 'I don't believe I'm hearing this,' she said. 'If you were going to get rid of her, you could have done it half an hour ago.'

'You don't understand, Grace. If you value your job, you will come back with me now.'

Value her job? What on earth was going on? She should

be panicking, but instead it was Mitch who looked distraught. This was too important to discuss from a sitting position. She swung her legs out of the car and jumped to her feet, her hands planting themselves on her hips to underline her indignation. 'My job depends on my going back to that table? To be put down by that witch?'

His dark eyes bored into hers. 'More or less.'

Why wasn't she terrified? Her work meant everything to her. Surely this should be a moment of pure dread? But all she could feel was hot, volcanic, exploding anger. 'If these are the new job specifications you and the delightful Candy have come up with, then it's time for me to make an important career move.'

'What are you talking about?'

'What am I talking about, Mitch? Do I have to spell it out? I'm resigning.'

Mitch paled. 'Please, Grace. Don't do this to me. I've got too much happening at present. My whole company's at risk. I don't think I have time to deal with your emotional outbursts as well.'

'You *rat*!' She was within a hair's breadth of slapping his face.

'*Rat?*' He had the nerve to look shocked. 'I'm a *rat*?'

First Roger, and now Mitch. She couldn't believe history was repeating itself. 'A shallow, materialistic, bully-boy rat.' The words flowed from the bitter resentment pouring through her. To hell with men! 'You couldn't care less about me, except as a useful—useful commodity.'

'Grace, don't overreact.' His hand reached out to her and she sprang back to avoid the contact.

Cruel memories of his hands on her skin and his passionate responses to her touch made her voice tremble. 'I believe my contract requires one month's notice. You've got it as from now.'

Blindly, she plunged back into the driver's seat, grabbed the door handle and yanked her door shut. She slammed it so savagely, she barely missed injuring Mitch.

'You don't understand...' he yelled.

Ignoring his protests, she angrily thrust her key into the ignition, jammed her foot on the accelerator and launched the gear lever into reverse. And as she screeched and roared out of the car park she had a brief glimpse of Mitch in her rearview mirror, looking chalky white and horrified.

Good, she told herself. We've finally set things straight.

## CHAPTER ELEVEN

THE sealed envelope, clearly identified by the jaunty green and aqua Tropicana logo, was waiting on Grace's desk when she returned from morning tea. She had been expecting Mitch's response to her letter of resignation, but that didn't stop her stomach from tightening when she saw it sitting there. Since she'd roared out of the hotel car park a few days ago, her insides had been twisted into permanent knots and now the strong coffee she'd just drunk churned unpleasantly.

With trembling hands, she reached for the envelope and slit it with her paper knife. When she extracted its contents, her hand shook so badly, she couldn't read the words on the page.

*This is ridiculous.* She closed her eyes and took a deep breath. Just read the letter and then you can get on with your life!

She placed the paper on her desk, lowered herself into her chair, and slowly spread the single page out flat. Then she read it through carefully.

> Tropicana Films
> Northtown Centre
> Flinders Mall

July 8th

Dear Ms Robbins,

As you requested, I am responding to your letter of resignation with a written reply. I also note that your decision to leave this company is unconditional in that you are not prepared to discuss any counter-offers for the retention of your services.

Naturally, I have no alternative but to accept your resignation. However, I do so most reluctantly. You are aware of the terms of your contract, which require four weeks' notice by either party. It is my wish, as Managing Director, that you continue your duties until August 6th.

As you know, the future of *New Tomorrow* will be decided within the next few weeks and it is imperative that all staff engaged on this vital project apply themselves totally to their immediate tasks in a completely professional manner.

Your work as Executive Assistant to the Managing Director has, until your sudden and untimely resignation, always been of the highest professional standard and I need you to maintain this level of commitment in the next four weeks before you leave us.

Yours faithfully,
*M.J. Wentworth*
Mitchell J. Wentworth
Managing Director

She read it through twice, one hand over her mouth and the other pressed hard against her pounding chest. So this was it. The end of the job she cherished.

And goodbye to the man she'd been foolish enough to imagine she loved.

Her eyes closed to squeeze back the threat of tears, but images of a glowing campfire, a canopy of outback stars and a sexy, masculine smile invaded her mind. Grace pressed her lips together to hold back a bitter sob. She hurt so much, she wanted to run away. Now. To get out of the office. Out of North Queensland. Anywhere, as long as she was able to cut free.

'But he won't let me leave,' she whispered to the empty office. 'Not yet. I have to stay here four more weeks.'

Four weeks! How could she bear it? She had expected that Mitch would have been eager to let her go. She'd half expected him to demand that she clear her desk that very minute.

A tap on her door sent her spinning around.

Maria hovered in the office doorway, her arms full of papers and her eyes wide with concern. 'I was just bringing those printouts you asked for,' she said uncertainly.

Grace sniffed and blinked, hoping her face showed no sign of tears. 'That's great. Thanks.' She held out one hand for the papers and tried to cover Mitch's letter with the other, but she knew she'd been caught out.

'You've heard from the boss, haven't you?' came her friend's predictable query.

Grace nodded. 'He won't let me go straight away. I have to work out the four weeks of my notice.'

'The insensitive brute!' Maria accompanied her outburst with a thump of her fist as she dropped the printouts onto Grace's desk.

'He paid me some kind of back-handed compliment about my professionalism,' explained Grace, feeling strengthened by Maria's support, but then her face crumpled. 'He wasn't too worried about being professional when we were…'

'When you were playing Swiss Family Robinson with him up in the Gulf country?' supplied Maria. 'No need to blush and look embarrassed, Grace. I'm sure Mr. W. is too much temptation for any woman. Even you. What I don't understand is why you two came back fighting. Or is it just that your return coincided with Ms Sorbell's arrival?'

Grace sighed. She couldn't deny that Candy was a part, or perhaps the whole of her problem. 'Mitch doesn't give a hoot for me as a person. He just wants me as someone who has a finger on all the important pulses. You know— logistics, locations—all the things I was putting into place before he arrived.'

Feeling strengthened by her growing anger, Grace picked up the memo she'd received from Mitch the previous day, outlining tasks to be completed. She shook it at Maria. 'If it's professionalism he wants, he'll get four weeks of professionalism like he's never seen before. If this project falls over, it won't be because of anything I've done; it'll be because Mitch Wentworth's ego is too big.'

'Way to go,' cheered Maria. 'You show him. He'll certainly get a shock when he tries to replace you.'

'I doubt it.' Grace sighed, slumping back into her chair and fingering Mitch's letter. She began folding it into a tiny wad.

Maria backed towards the door. 'He's so tied up with his Candy stick, he wouldn't have a clue what you've put in place. All the details about the army, the accommodation for the cast and crew, caterers, charter flights, helicopters. The poor fool doesn't know it, but after you leave, Grace, our mighty Mitch Wentworth is going to find himself standing in the middle of an empty set with a puzzled look, scratching his cute behind.'

'Miss Cavalero?'

The jaws of both women dropped in the direction of their knees as a dark, masculine shape filled the doorway. Maria's face raced through three shades of red till it reached purple. 'M-Mr Wentworth?' she stammered.

With his mouth clenched in a grim, tight line, Mitch

inclined his head ever so slightly in the direction of his office down the corridor. 'A word, please.'

'Yes, sir.'

'In my office. I'll be with you in a moment.'

Maria shot a guilty glance in Grace's direction and backed out of the room. Before she scurried down the corridor, she paused behind Mitch's back and gestured a throat-slitting motion with her hand.

Under other circumstances, Grace might have been tempted to smile at her friend's antics, but not when Mitch remained in her office, stern-faced and bristling with tension.

'I need a list of all the contacts we have with the region's top business operators,' he ordered tersely.

'That won't take long,' Grace replied, making a supreme effort to keep her voice businesslike. 'I have them all on file.'

She expected him to nod curtly and leave her. When he remained standing beside her chair, his unsmiling eyes resting on her, Grace pressed shaking fingers to her lips.

Mitch spoke softly. 'I'm completely tied up with a number of financial negotiations at present, but when these matters are settled we need to talk.'

She gulped. 'To discuss the arrival of the cast and the first shooting sessions?'

Mitch sighed and ran impatient fingers through his hair. 'No, Grace, it wasn't the movie business that I wanted to discuss.'

'Oh?' For just a second or two, she saw a flash of pain in his dark, stormy eyes. Her heart exploded as his gaze held hers. Surely she only imagined that Mitch looked hurt and lonely?

Without warning, his hand reached out to cup her chin and his head lowered until his mouth pressed urgently against hers. It was the shortest, hottest, most breathtaking kiss she'd ever experienced. 'We have other unfinished business,' he muttered heatedly into her ear. His thumb stroked her throat just once, and her skin flamed at his touch.

Then Mitch turned abruptly and was gone.

Grace did her level best to forget about that high-voltage kiss over the days that followed, but in spite of her efforts unexpected memories of the heated pressure of his mouth against hers would jump out and torment her. Then other taunting memories would follow.

Blast the man! If Mitch thought he could accept her resignation and still take liberties with her body, he was in for a surprise! She kept herself busy, convinced that hard work was the only thing between her sanity and a nervous breakdown. It helped that she saw very little of her boss. He and Candy and, on occasion, the company's accountant seemed to be involved in endless discussions behind firmly closed doors.

During the day, Grace coped by working flat out at the office, and in the evening she voraciously read overseas tourist brochures. What she needed, as soon as she was released from this job, was to get as far away as possible from Mitchell J. Wentworth.

The more inaccessible and remote the destinations, the more they interested her. Places like the Himalayas, Scotland's Orkney Isles or a trip up the Amazon had distinct appeal. But after a week of avid reading she was depressed to realise that these far-flung places might be no help at all.

When she sat at her desk and reflected that the attraction of these locations lay in their beautiful natural environments, Grace was plagued by a fresh crop of paralysing doubts. Wouldn't it be terrible if she travelled all the way across the globe only to spend her time thinking about some place else—an isolated spot with wide open skies and a pool carved out of a rocky platform?

A corner of her mouth curled in self-ridicule.

Perhaps she should find a big city to hide in. Buenos Aires? Tokyo? New York? But there was every chance that her memories would follow her there, too. Would she jump out of her skin every time she saw a tall, dark and handsome man?

A clinking of jewellery nearby brought Grace out of her daydream. The sound of Candy's bracelet was now infamous throughout the building. Only yesterday Maria had commented that the rattling charms warned everybody of her approach in much the same manner as the ticking clock swallowed by the crocodile in *Peter Pan*.

As the sound came closer, Grace looked up from her desk to see Candy sailing through her doorway, bringing a cloud of perfume with her. 'I've just popped in to say goodbye,' she said, helping herself to a chair.

Grace's eyes widened as she swung round to face Candy. 'Oh, really? I had no idea you were leaving already.' She was also very surprised that this high flier would bother to deliver a personal farewell to her.

'I've been here over a week, honey.' Candy crossed one shapely leg over the other and began to swing her foot. 'And I've completed my business.'

'And it was successful?' Grace queried, although she hardly expected Candy to take her into her confidence at this late stage.

The other woman's eyes glazed over and her leg stopped swinging. For a moment she looked as wooden as a mannequin in a shop window. Then she flashed Grace an ultra bright smile. 'In business terms, it was a complete and unmitigated failure.'

'A failure?' echoed Grace with a frown. 'I don't understand.'

'It's quite simple. Apart from the personal pleasure of—' she offered a simpering smile '—of catching up with our mutual friend, Mitch, my trip here has been a fiasco. Your darling boss has been playing financial games with me and he won. I lost. End of story.'

As Candy's leg began its imitation of a pendulum once more, Grace's heartbeats picked up pace. 'I'm still confused. I guess this means High Sierra won't be giving Tropicana any financial backing. How does that make Mitch a winner?'

Candy leaned forward conspiratorially. 'Because he snaffled a better deal, Gracie. He's been putting together some other negotiations behind my back, and now he's played his trump card. He's getting all the funds he wants from the Queensland Film Commission.'

'Wow! That's fantastic!' For a reckless moment, Grace forgot completely that she wasn't part of this company's future. All she could think of was how relieved Mitch would be to have the rest of the money he needed, and on his terms.

Candy nodded glumly. 'The Commission has agreed to give Tropicana the additional finance plus plenty of help with promotion. Understandably, they are excited about a blockbuster Australian movie filmed on location in North Queensland.'

'I guess so,' Grace agreed, but she was feeling utterly miserable again. She had to face the reality that the person who took her place would inherit a really exciting job.

Candy jumped to her feet and began to pace the room. 'I tried to tell my boss at High Sierra he was crazy holding out for fifty-one per cent, when all Mitch wanted to negotiate was twenty. I did my best to convince Joe that Mitch is no fool and that we'd be better off grabbing the twenty per cent because it would be twenty per cent of a big winner.'

'I'm surprised that you're taking the time to tell me all this. You know I won't be sticking with this project, don't you? I've handed in my resignation.'

'Yeah.' The other woman stopped pacing and stood squarely in the centre of the room with her feet apart, eyeing Grace. 'And I just wanted to say I think you're very wise to leave this company.'

A confusing heat crept into Grace's cheeks. Why should Candy applaud her leaving a winning project? Unless… 'Why should you care where I work?' she challenged.

Crossing her arms across her chest, Candy narrowed her eyes. 'We gals have got to stick together.'

'I see,' murmured Grace doubtfully. What she actually suspected was that Candy had a king-size crush on Mitch. The American had made no secret of her admiration for their wonder-boy boss. The whole office knew about it. Grace toyed with a pen on her desk. 'Am I also to understand that you might—*care*—for Mr Wentworth?'

With an exasperated sigh, Candy plonked herself back into the chair opposite Grace, crossed her legs and began the swinging once more. 'I'll be brutally frank with you, Gracie.'

*Ouch!* People usually used that term when they wanted to say something hurtful.

'Mitch Wentworth and I go back a long way.' Candy blew out air in the same way a smoker expels smoke from a cigarette.

What had happened to her own ability to breathe? Grace wondered. Her chest was painfully tight.

'We've always had a special—*understanding*,' continued Candy.

Unable to look at Candy, Grace made a show of studying her fingernails. She couldn't let the other woman see how much her words hurt. Her voice wobbled as she snapped a hasty retort. 'This special relationship you claim to have didn't help you secure the deal.'

Candy released a self-mocking little chuckle. 'Business and personal affairs are not good bedmates. But you'd understand that, wouldn't you, Gracie?'

Feeling as if she'd just stepped off a rollercoaster, Grace struggled to take in the implications of Candy's question. The floor beneath her seemed to sway and lurch. 'Mitch and I aren't having—'

'Hold it right there, honey. Don't protest too much. I've seen the way you look at your boss. And remember, I've known the dear boy for a long, long time. I understand his little *weaknesses*.' Candy's swinging foot stopped in mid-air and she used it to point at Grace. 'Don't think I blame you for making the most of a golden opportunity.'

'What on earth do you mean?'

'Getting yourself lost with Mitch in the bush. That was cute, real cute.'

Horrified by what Candy was implying, Grace jumped to her feet. 'You think I planned that? Risked my life just to—just to—'

'Climb into the sack with a babe like Mitch?' Candy

favoured Grace with a knowing smirk. 'It was worth it, wasn't it, Gracie?'

Her fist clenched and, for an insane moment, Grace could feel it landing on Candy Sorbell's pert nose with a satisfying crunch. Struggling to keep her voice steady, she replied, 'What are you hoping to achieve by trying to dig up this dirt?'

The other woman's eyebrow arched. 'Why, honey, I'm offering you some sisterly advice.' She got up, crossed the room and placed both hands on Grace's shoulders, shaking her gently. 'However *sweet* Mitch was when you guys were alone in the outback, he's shown his true feelings for you by accepting your resignation without so much as a whimper. Don't waste any energy hankering after the man, my dear. I bet he was something else out there in the back of beyond, but, believe me, it was a flash in the pan.'

As if she sensed Grace's fury, Candy moved away, but hovered in the office doorway. 'Most of the women Mitch dates have the shelf-life of a punnet of fresh strawberries. Honestly, sweetheart, he wouldn't settle seriously for a quiet little thing like you. So, congratulations, you're doing the right thing by getting clear away.'

With another jangle of her jewellery, Candy left, and Grace lowered herself stiffly into her chair, staring into space.

Her ears recorded the sound of Candy's high heels tapping their exit along the corridor and somewhere a telephone was ringing. But echoing over and over in Grace's head were the words Candy had uttered: 'He wouldn't settle seriously for a quiet little thing like you.'

She knew it was true. It was what she'd told herself many times. Despite everything that had happened at the rock pool, Mitch didn't care about her as a person. He'd proved that by dropping her and turning to Candy, without so much as a backward glance. All he wanted from her now was a highly efficient assistant with a finger on all the important pulses.

And, while she knew she could search the world over without finding another man capable of capturing her heart and soul as completely as he had, Grace was just as aware that replacing her was a cinch for Mitch.

All he had to do was advertise her position in one of the country's major newspapers.

# CHAPTER TWELVE

GRACE was emotionally exhausted when she dragged herself back to her office the next morning. What had appalled her and kept her awake all night was the dreadful sense of revisiting the past—discovering all over again her unerring talent for falling in love with rats.

For the past week, while she'd worried about Mitch's interest in Candy, she'd been sick with misery. But a stubborn part of her mind had clung to the fragile hope that perhaps she'd imagined everything wrongly. Perhaps Mitch was only humouring Candy in order to clinch the deal. But yesterday Candy had spelt out just how *intimate* she and Mitch had been, and that was unbearable.

For just a moment she'd been tempted to disregard Candy's claims as jealous gossip, but three-year-old memories brought her back to reality. All the pain came flooding back. She had been so sure Roger loved her, yet he'd had no compunction about flinging her aside in his rush to scale the heady heights of business. Now she'd learned her lesson. She'd been taken in once by a handsome, sexy, successful man who'd left her feeling used and crushed. She wasn't going to let it happen again.

The sound of impatient footsteps forced her to lift her head and she groaned softly when she saw the current rat in her life marching stiffly through her doorway.

'Grace,' Mitch barked.

She felt like suggesting he get lost again—*permanently* this time—but, to her chagrin, Grace found her heart beginning to thump and she was jumping to attention. 'Yes, Mr Wentworth?'

He frowned and repeated, '*Grace,*' clearly emphasising his use of her first name, 'can we try again for dinner?'

The sheaf of papers she was holding fluttered to the floor with a soft swish, like pigeons landing. 'Oh, no,' she whispered, and bent to retrieve them.

A firm hand on her arm stopped her. 'I'll get them.' Mitch snatched the papers together impatiently and tossed them onto her desk. 'Well?'

'Dinner? Mitch, for heaven's sake, whatever for?'

Mitch gaped at her as if he couldn't believe what he'd heard. 'I had this weird idea that we could sit at a table and cut up food with a knife and fork. Then, after an amount of chewing and swallowing, I'd expect digestion to take place. The idea—'

'Sarcasm doesn't suit you,' she cut in, wishing she could sit down. Any minute now her knees would give way.

'No? I'm sorry, but I've had an awful week and I find your question frustrating. Why on earth wouldn't we have dinner? We need to talk.'

Grace noticed then how pale and drawn Mitch looked, and a painful lump clogged her throat. Trying to conceal her shaking hands, she folded her arms tightly across her chest. 'Mitch, I—' she struggled to reply '—I'm leaving soon. Do you really think it's wise for us to get together again?'

His expression softened slightly. 'I am sure it would be very unwise if we were to part without a decent chance to discuss—everything.'

Oh, why was she so weak? She could think of nothing nicer than going out to dinner with him. An image of Mitch, escorting her through an elegant restaurant to an intimate table for two danced through her imagination. She could picture him looking dark and dashing, pulling out her chair for her, smiling at her as they surveyed the menu together.

Grace pressed her lips together tightly to hold back the urge to accept his invitation. And she forced her mind to focus on the pain of Candy's revelations.

'I'm told there's an interesting garden restaurant in South Townsville,' he continued. 'I know the nights are cool, but it's still pleasant enough to eat outdoors. Will you join me tomorrow evening?'

'I—I'm busy tomorrow evening—it's late-night shopping.'

Mitch shoved his hands in his pockets and rocked on his heels. 'You'll have to come up with a better excuse than that.'

'Mitch, I don't think we should.'

'You've got to come out with me, Grace. I know it's unfortunate that I had to wait till Candy left.'

*Good grief! How could he talk so calmly to her about Candy? He must have had his conscience surgically removed.* She swung her head away and stared fiercely at her filing cabinet and tried counting to ten. 'You want me to take over where Ms Sorbell left off?'

'Pardon?'

Drawing in a deep breath, she swivelled back to face him. 'There's absolutely nothing personal left for us to discuss.'

He opened his mouth to protest, but she rushed on, not giving him a chance to hurt her even more. 'And, in case you've forgotten, I've resigned. I'm giving you another three weeks of professionalism and then I'm out of here.' With a grand sweeping gesture she pointed to the door. '*And* I very much doubt that dinner with you would aid my digestion.'

Mitch shook his head, clearly puzzled. 'What's going on here? Why are you so hung up about Candy?'

*Hung up? His liaison with another woman was a minor issue?*

The man had the moral habits of a rabbit! With every ounce of will-power, Grace ignored his question. 'I saw something come through on a fax yesterday afternoon about the launch of *New Tomorrow* being brought forward.'

'Grace, don't change the subject.'

'Is that correct? The State Minister for Tourism and the Arts will be in town next Thursday?'

'Damn it, Grace!'

Inhaling a deep breath, she forced herself to calm down. 'Mitch, I have nothing of a personal nature I wish to discuss with you.'

His hands rose as if he was about to grip her shoulders. For agonising moments, he stood facing her, his hands inches from connection.

'If I have to get a launch together in just a few days,' she continued, her voice tight with the effort to sound businesslike, 'I need to find out exactly what has to be done.'

For a long, breathless silence, Mitch stood still as stone and stared at her, then he sighed heavily and dropped his gaze to the grey carpet on her office floor. One hand kneaded his forehead as if he had a headache.

After more moments of silence, he looked up again and spoke. 'Okay, Grace, if this is the way you want it, I'll play it your way for now. The government has come through with the funding we need and the Minister doesn't want to miss the chance to promote his generosity before the media. So yes, we should launch the project while he's here.'

She swallowed, trying to shift the heavy lump of hopelessness lodged in her throat. She felt as if she'd swallowed a golf ball. 'It will be quite a challenge to pull all that together by next Thursday.'

Mitch nodded his agreement. 'I know, but the Minister's press staff are looking after notifying the media. We just have to throw together an invitation list for local VIPs and tee up a suitable venue.'

'Are you bringing up any of the cast?' It was hard to believe she could do this—keep talking about business while her heart was slowly breaking up, chunk by bleeding chunk.

'Of course, we definitely need our stars. They'll draw plenty of attention.'

'It'll be tricky, but I think we should just be able to pull a function like that together in time,' she told him, but she was speaking on automatic pilot, as if her head and her heart were disconnected.

'I'm sure you'll do an excellent job as always, Grace.' Mitch took three steps towards the door and turned. 'Thank you.'

She moved over to her desk, as if she expected him to head off and leave her to get on with her work now the discussion was over.

But he remained there, watching her. 'Grace, whatever you might have heard about me or decided about me, I'm actually not—'

'You want the invitations sent out first thing this morning?'

His splayed hand thumped her office wall. 'What are you made of, woman? Petrified wood?'

*If only she were!* She lifted her chin and told him boldly, 'I'm one hundred per cent old-fashioned common sense.'

At that, Mitch muttered a curse and strode out of the room.

And after he left, Grace stared at the empty doorway,

feeling numb, as if her entire body had been anaesthetised from the eyebrows down. Why was Mitch so angry? How could he possibly expect her to go out to dinner with him and, presumably, take up where Candy left off? He knew she wasn't the type for a casual on-again, off-again affair.

How long she stood there she wasn't sure, but she was still in exactly the same position when Mitch came charging back.

'Here's the list of people we need to fly in for the launch.' He thrust a sheet of paper under her nose.

'Great. Thanks,' she replied dully, while her eyes skimmed the names listed in his spiky handwriting. One name jumped out at her. '*George Hervey?* You're inviting him?'

'Yeah. Your old mentor and number one fan. Surely you haven't got a problem with *that*?'

Horrified, she shook the page at Mitch. 'Of course I have. You can't invite George. It would be awful for him.'

He stared at her with the same stunned expression he might have worn if she'd accused him of kidnapping Santa Claus. 'Why shouldn't George be part of the celebration?'

'For heaven's sake, Mitch! How could you be so mean? Why do you have to rub poor George's nose in your own success?'

Bursting with moral indignation, Grace threw her hands in the air. How could Mitch be so insensitive? 'Wasn't it bad enough that you railroaded your way into the company with your bully-boy take-over bid? You threw George out to pasture. At the very least you could leave him in peace.'

'Grace, I will not be yelled at.'

She blinked as she realised just how loud her voice had become, and dropped her tone several decibels. 'George treated me almost like a daughter. Can't you see how terrible this would be for the poor man?'

Talk about coming back to earth! With the speed of a pricked party balloon, her very last, fragile hope about Mitch's integrity lay, deflated and shrivelled, at her feet. It was one thing for him to flit from woman to woman as the fancy took him, but how could he be so mean-spirited? How could he invite the man whose business he'd commandeered to witness his own hour of triumph?

Mitch was looking thunderous. 'I guess it's fair to say that, in your opinion, I've made an error of judgement.'

Grace whirled around. 'I'm completely shocked.'

'George doesn't have to accept the invitation.'

'Of course he does. He has his pride.' She stared at the ceiling, shaking her head. 'But I can't understand you, Mitch. You're either totally vindictive and egotistical or completely insensitive. Either way, you're not the kind of man I could ever lo—' Just in time she clamped her mouth shut.

'What was that, Grace? Were you about to mention— *love*?' He stepped towards her, his intense gaze lancing her, stripping away the protective shield of her anger.

Grace gulped, squirming under his probing stare, and she tried to pretend she hadn't heard that word, but she knew her cheeks were blazing.

'Were you about to admit—' His voice cracked dangerously '—that you—that we have something special going?'

She shook her head. 'I—I—' Totally flustered, she attacked from a different angle. 'What is it with men? Why do you all have to be so—so vicious? You seem to relish waging corporate warfare.'

But for some reason, Mitch wasn't glaring at her any more. He relaxed against her filing cabinet and folded his arms casually across his chest. 'So you think we're all brutes in suits?'

In desperation, her voice rose again. 'You bought out

this company and now you want to parade poor old George like some kind of battle trophy.'

'Another male strikes a blow for his own ego?' suggested Mitch with the hint of a smile.

'How can you joke about this? It's disastrous.'

What was so disastrous was the obvious fact that Mitch was just as selfish as she had always feared.

'Hang on, Grace, I think you have a rather personalised view of disaster.' The old teasing glint was back in Mitch's eyes. He glanced at his watch. 'Look, I really don't have time to argue the toss with you. I have a corporation or two to raid.'

She sniffed at his flippant rejection of her well-placed criticism.

'So,' he continued, 'I'll leave you to issue George Hervey with an invitation, and, as you have such a special relationship with the dear fellow and you're so worried about his fragile ego, if he accepts, I want *you* to be his personal escort at the launch.'

Without so much as a by-your-leave, Mitch strode swiftly out of her office once more. Grace didn't close her mouth until some time after he had left.

# CHAPTER THIRTEEN

CHAMPAGNE corks popped. Glasses clinked and cameras flashed.

Beneath feathery palm trees, laughter and light-hearted chatter floated on the warm, tropical winter air as guests met and mingled at the poolside reception area.

The launch of *New Tomorrow* was in full swing.

At the entry to the hotel's pool area, Grace acted as hostess, greeting guests and handing out promotional packages. The celebrity stars had arrived and were being fussed over by the local mayor and other city dignitaries.

Out of the corner of her eye, she watched Mitch circulating, soaking up the back-slaps and the hearty congratulations and smiling charmingly at the furiously batting feminine eyelashes. In his sleek suit, crisp shirt and silk tie, he was looking his corporate best.

Almost all the region's top business people had turned up, but, to Grace's relief, although George Hervey had accepted the invitation, he had not made an appearance. Perhaps he'd changed his mind.

She could almost relax.

Checking her watch, she reassured herself that everything was running to schedule. Waiters circulated with huge silver platters offering a range of cheeses and dainty seafood combinations served on water crackers. A suitably eager pack of journalists and photographers panted around the speakers' podium, angling their cameras and thrusting their microphones forward.

Finally, the Minister, looking as dignified and pompous

as an opera star about to burst into his favourite aria, moved onto the podium to address the crowd. 'The making of *New Tomorrow* is a sound investment for the people of this state,' he boomed, and his arm extended to acknowledge Mitch, who had joined him.

'This project is a fine example of the great partnership that can be achieved between our government and the private sector.'

In the manner of all politicians, phrases glowing with promise rolled off his tongue and his florid face deepened in colour as he warmed to his topic.

Grace circled around the edge of the crowd, checking that all was well. Drinks waiters were standing by, ready to top up people's glasses for the toasts. And as soon as the speeches were over, hot savouries would be served. Everything seemed in order.

Except her. She longed to escape. What she wanted most was to hang a sign around her neck stating, 'Out of order' or 'Gone fishing'.

If only she could vanish. This revelry was proving much more of an ordeal than she had anticipated. She was the only person present who had nothing to celebrate. Before the first scene of this movie could be shot, she would be gone.

Luckily, over the past week, since she'd discovered just exactly what kind of corporate commando Mitch was, she had hardly seen him.

Everyone in the company had been swarming frantically backwards and forwards, from one task to the next, like distracted ants. Mitch's casual assumption that a launch could be pulled together in a matter of days without much disruption had been another example of his supreme arrogance.

But they had done it. The launch was happening.

And with that behind them she would be able to say goodbye to Tropicana Films and Mitchell J. Wentworth once and for all.

But the prospect of leaving still hurt.

Coming to terms with the realisation that she had pegged Mitch correctly from the start was the hardest lesson of her life. Perhaps one day she would be able to rid herself of this gnawing sense of loss. One day her head would find a way to teach her heart to stop pounding whenever he or his company or his movies were mentioned.

She could rationalise it all in her mind. The facts spoke for themselves. Mitch was so handsome, charming and sexy that he could believe his own hype and forget about the feelings of others. But when would her heart accept this reality? When would she be able to forget about the other, tender and tantalising side of Mitch? When…?

'Grace!'

Someone whispering her name brought her swivelling around, and her old boss's kind and familiar face came into focus. 'George!'

'How are you, my dear?'

Looking more frail than she remembered, the elderly and balding George Hervey flung a fatherly arm around her shoulders and gave her a peck on the cheek.

'It's so good to see you,' she whispered. 'I thought you'd changed your mind about coming.'

'Plane was delayed taking off from Mascot,' George explained. 'What's this fellow rambling on about?' He squinted towards the Minister on the podium. 'Let's get out of here and you can tell me your news. I never did like political speeches.' George took Grace's hand and drew her towards a door leading out of the pool area.

Happy to escape, she followed without a murmur. And, as they hurried away, George said, 'You're looking more beautiful than ever, Grace. Working for Mitch must agree with you.'

How courageous this man is, she thought. Here he is, cut to the core over his loss of Tropicana Films, and he takes time to pay me compliments. All her protective instincts sprang into high gear. And, once the glass doors cut them off from the crowd, she turned to her old friend. 'George, you're a brave man.'

'I am?' he replied with a puzzled smile.

'Of course you are. I couldn't believe Mitch made you come here today. And I don't blame you at all for wanting to escape the celebrations. All that chest-beating and trumpet-blowing. It's offensive.'

'Some of the speeches can be tedious,' George agreed. 'But I'll go back out there when Mitch talks. I want to hear what he has to say.'

'Oh, no, you don't.'

'Why not? Have you heard Mitch speak? I can't imagine he would be boring.'

'But it will be so painful for you, George.'

George looked puzzled. 'My dear, I'm feeling perfectly well. I'm quite fit actually, even if I do look a bit decrepit.'

'Oh, I don't mean physically painful. I mean emotionally...' Grace brought her hand to her heart. 'You must be feeling so hurt—so distressed and—and resentful.'

'You're confusing me, Grace. Come and sit down.'

They headed for some deep cane chairs in the hotel foyer.

'Can I get you something to drink—a cup of tea, perhaps?' she asked.

'No, no. I'll eat and drink my fill when I go back out there in a minute. Now, tell me how things are going for you.'

Grace tossed a grand gesture in the direction of the celebrations beyond the huge wall of glass. 'Tropicana is the name on everyone's lips!'

George leaned forward. 'But how are you, Grace? Are you happy?'

Hesitating to tell too much, she twisted her hands together. 'I wish I was still working for you,' she said at last. When she looked up, she was surprised to see George looking pale and anxious.

'But, my dear, you wouldn't have a job.'

Grace frowned. 'What are you talking about?'

'There'd be no Tropicana Films.'

'That's rubbish.'

George took off his glasses and polished them with his handkerchief. He blinked myopically at Grace. 'I was sure the news would have filtered through by now—about the mess I made of the company.'

'M-m-mess?'

'A dreadful mess, my dear. I made some extremely unwise decisions and managed to let Tropicana fall into bad shape. Very bad shape indeed. If it wasn't for Mitch Wentworth rescuing the company when it was on the verge of bankruptcy, there would be no Tropicana Films.'

At Grace's gasp of astonishment, he patted her hand and nodded. 'The dear boy took a huge gamble and invested his life's savings to bale me out.'

'But he…but he…' She groped for words with the desperation of someone drowning, but was forced to give up. 'You were *happy* for him to take over?'

'Deliriously.' George replaced his spectacles and his blue eyes blazed with certainty. 'I was facing financial ruin and the threat of a poverty-stricken old age. I'm indebted to Mitch and I'm just so relieved that it looks like he'll make a go of it.'

She stared back at George, shaking her head. 'But why

didn't he explain all that to me? He's known all along that I believed he'd bullied you into selling out.'

'He never said anything?'

Grace shook her head again. She felt confused, guilty... ill.

'I guess he didn't want to broadcast my failure. He's a gentleman, Grace.'

'No, he's not,' she retorted automatically. 'He can't be. He...'

George looked a little shamefaced. 'I'm really sorry I didn't explain all this to you at the time. But a man has his pride. You looked up to me, and I'm afraid I was rather weak. I took the coward's way out and just crept quietly away. I didn't want to see your disappointment.'

'Oh, George.' Grace left her chair and stooped to give him a hug. 'I wouldn't have thought any the worse of you.' She sighed heavily. 'But I might have thought just a little more highly of my new boss.'

George patted her arm. 'It's a pity that you and he haven't hit it off. I've been nursing a secret fantasy that you two are a perfect match.'

'Really? What a ridiculous notion.' Grace could feel a blush coming on. Quickly, she tried to change the subject. 'You said you wanted to hear Mitch's speech. Perhaps you'd better go back.'

George's news had rocked her completely. Needing a chance to take it all in, she dragged him out of his chair and almost pushed him towards the pool area.

She desperately wanted time to think.

As she watched George go, Grace felt all at sea. Disoriented. It was as if her understanding of north and south, right and wrong, truth and falsehood had broken loose—leaving her to drift without a chart.

*Mitch's take-over had been a rescue?*

She remembered his stunned expression when she'd harangued him mercilessly about his mistreatment of George.

*The male corporate raider was a gentleman?*

She stood stiffly, watching through the glass, following George's stooped figure as he mingled with the crowd. And in the distance she could see Mitch at the microphone, smiling, waving his hand to acknowledge the applause. She watched the guests raise their glasses...heard the faint cheers...saw the cameras flashing...saw Mitch smiling... felt tears slide down her cheeks.

*Don't get too sentimental,* a warning inner voice whispered. *Remember Candy.*

But somehow Candy's accusations had a hollow ring to them now. Mitch had always claimed bewilderment whenever she'd dropped hints about Candy.

*Perhaps...*

Grabbing tissues from her shoulder bag, she mopped at her face and began to walk forward slowly.

*Perhaps...*

She had to speak to him.

Predictably, by the time Grace drew near to Mitch, he was surrounded by a throng of well-wishers, who had rushed forward to shake his hand.

Standing to one side, she waited quietly, watching him while her heart raced. She watched him deliver his killer charm as effortlessly as he might spread jam on toast. A little lopsided smile here, a twinkle of the eye there. A polite laugh for one man's joke, concentrated attention for another's more serious comments.

Then he saw her.

Her chest tightened unbearably as his dark eyes locked onto hers.

The group clustered around him continued to gush and chatter, but Mitch stared straight at Grace. For a brief second, his eyes wandered vaguely to a woman who was trying to ask him a question, but Grace saw him offer an excuse.

As he continued to watch her closely, Mitch separated from the crowd and made his way towards her.

Her heart drummed.

'You were wanting to speak to me?' he asked.

# CHAPTER FOURTEEN

Now her knees knocked together. She needed to run into Mitch's arms. To apologise—to ask a thousand questions.

He was so tall, so dangerously, dreamily beautiful.

Single-handed, he'd rescued Tropicana Films.

'I—I need to speak to you about one of the guests, Mr Wentworth,' she said, in the most businesslike voice she could manage.

Mitch glanced at a gaggle of bystanders, queuing to meet him. 'Right now, Ms Robbins?'

'If you'd be so kind.' She tried to keep her face impassive, but was defeated by the fat tear that filled her right eye.

He frowned. And, for a heart-wrenching moment, he hesitated and glanced again at the throng waiting to speak to him. And she imagined he was considering refusing her request. But then he turned politely to the line of people gathered behind him. 'If you'll excuse me,' he murmured, 'I need to consult with my executive assistant.'

Grace saw a waiter coming from the kitchen with a fresh plate of crispy Chinese chicken wings. She beckoned to him. 'These people are hungry,' she said, indicating the group Mitch had been speaking to, and he hastily moved to serve them. Fortunately they murmured appreciatively.

Stepping towards Grace, Mitch placed a hand at the small of her back and steered her away from the crowd.

'Can we go somewhere private?' she asked, then bit her lip anxiously.

His eyes widened with surprise, but to her relief he nod-

168

ded and turned towards the far end of the pool. As they walked, his hand stayed at her back and she sensed its warmth through the fine linen of her blouse.

He didn't speak till they reached a rectangle of grass screened off from the crowds by clusters of golden cane palms.

Suddenly hopelessly nervous, Grace came to an abrupt halt. She turned to stare at the peaceful view across Cleveland Bay. In the distance, she could make out the faint blue humps of the Palm Islands.

Mitch spoke quietly. 'You implied you have something important to discuss?'

She sucked in a deep breath of sea air, searching for a way to voice what needed to be said—that she'd been wrong about him and that she was sorry. 'I—I think I owe you an apology.'

Her words were gabbled and for a moment he looked startled. Then his hands rose to rest on his hips, pushing aside the elegant Italian suit coat. 'Do you, now?' His jaw relaxed and his face broke into a slow, teasing smile. 'Have you encountered the first step in my five-point plan?'

'The problem is,' Grace rushed on, shifting her line of sight from the gleam in his eye to a cloud drifting across the patch of afternoon sky beyond his right shoulder, 'I've kept thinking of you as...' She paused. 'Five-point-plan? What are you talking about?'

'I'll explain in due course. A man has to take precautions with you, Grace. But don't get sidetracked. You were talking about an apology. I'm intrigued.'

Grace squirmed, suddenly wary about baring her soul if Mitch still had something up his sleeve. 'But what's this five-point-plan?'

His head was cocked to one side, his expression bemused. 'My, my, you *are* impatient.'

'You've presented me with a puzzle, and I have one of those minds that likes to work things out.'

Mitch folded his arms across his chest and looked infuriatingly relaxed. 'It's the downside of being born with a brain. Now, let me hear why you dragged me away from my guests.'

'Oh,' she said, taking a deep breath. 'I've been talking to George Hervey.'

He regarded her steadily, but remained silent.

Her mouth twisted with the effort to hold back her nervousness. 'I think you knew that if George came here I would find out you didn't bulldoze him out of the way. That I've been holding a grudge against you—based on—not knowing the truth.'

Mitch's eyes glowed.

'What I'm trying to say is, I'm so sorry, Mitch. I was so rude to you. But how was I to know that you aren't a—a—?'

'A gold-plated rat?'

'Oh, Mitch.' Another tear rolled down her cheek.

With a soft sound, he reached out and gently traced the tear's path. 'I was certainly gambling on the fact that if you had a chance to speak to George, an intelligent woman like you could be trusted to put two and two together,' he murmured.

'And come up with point-number-one in this plan of yours?' she asked, curving her cheek closer into his touch.

He drew her nearer and chuckled as he lowered his face to hers. 'Yes, my clever Grace. That's exactly what I hoped.'

She shivered deliciously as their lips met.

There was an embarrassed cough behind them. 'Mr Wentworth?'

Mitch's head jerked back. 'What is it?'

'Er—the Minister will be leaving shortly, sir. He has another meeting to attend.'

'Yes, of course.' Mitch sighed. He looked at his watch. 'All right. I'm coming. Give me two minutes.'

As soon as the messenger had gone, Grace whispered, 'Two minutes? There are so many things I need to ask you.'
You could start with *Candy*, a warning voice niggled. But Grace didn't want to spoil this moment. Not when Mitch's dark eyes were sending her so many silent promises.

'I'm all ears. Fire away with your questions,' he said.

'We couldn't possibly get through points two to five in two minutes.'

He brushed his lips across her forehead. 'Patience, Grace.'

'I'm running out of patience,' she breathed.

'We don't want to rush something that's vitally important to get right.' He smiled and trailed slow, seductive kisses down her cheek. 'Will you promise not to disappear if I ask you to give me another hour? And then we'll discuss these matters in minute detail.' He sighed. 'But at the moment there are still a lot of people expecting to talk to me.'

Somehow she forced herself to reply. 'I suppose I could wait just a little longer.'

'I hope *I* can,' he murmured, dropping one last kiss behind her ear. 'And you'll promise to hang around?'

'Of course.'

They rejoined the crowd and, very quickly, Mitch was absorbed once more into the enthusiastic mood of the launch.

As soon as the Minister had been farewelled, Grace popped some snacks onto a plate for Mitch which he accepted with thanks and a wink, before continuing to discuss the brilliant quality of the natural light in North Queensland with a group of cameramen.

How can he stay so composed? she wondered as she mingled and chatted and tried to talk sense. She found it enormously difficult to concentrate on what people were saying. Especially as the whole time she conversed she was aware of Mitch, head and shoulders above the crowd.

He kept catching her eye and sending her knowing, secretive smiles. And each time her insides rippled with delight. But the ordeal of keeping up appearances for sixty long minutes was exhausting.

Eventually, as the sun began to dip into the sea, Maria appeared at her elbow. 'Grace, this arrived for you.' From behind her back, her friend produced a huge bouquet of flowers—beautiful native Australian wildflowers: wattles and banksias, grevilleas and wild irises.

Grace stared at the arrangement. 'They're beautiful. Are you sure they're for me and not for one of the stars?' she asked.

Maria shook her head. 'The fellow who delivered them insisted that they're for you. But the card's weird. No name on it. Just says "Point number two".'

'Oh,' Grace gasped.

'Oh?' queried Maria, studying her shrewdly. 'So you know who they're from?'

'Um, I have a fair idea.'

'Our esteemed boss tickling your fancy again?'

When Grace didn't answer, Maria added with a knowing smile, 'I have inside information that tells me things are looking good for you, Grace. But look at you! You're already bursting with…something.'

Grace smiled. It was no use trying to fool Maria. 'I was hoping it wasn't too obvious, but I'm so worked up, I feel like I'm about to explode.'

Maria cast a quick glance at her friend and then at the assembled guests. 'Can I suggest you implode? It's not as messy, and these people are all dressed up in their best bibs and tuckers.'

The two women burst into a fit of giggles.

For Grace, it was a relief to let off some of her pent-up emotion. Every part of her longed for Mitch, and yet she didn't know if she should dare to hope. All they really had between them were a few blissful days in the outback. Since then they'd done nothing but fight. And then, of course, there was the Candy factor.

'There's George Hervey,' commented Maria.

On the far side of the pool, Mitch and George were deep in conversation. And, as Grace watched, George gave Mitch a hearty pat on the back and the two men shook hands. There was a great deal of nodding and grinning and even some outright laughter. They were clearly on very good terms.

'Unless my eyes are deceiving me, our Mr W. can't be quite the black-hearted invader we imagined,' commented Maria.

Grace quickly explained what George had told her.

'Phew!' Maria whistled, before giving Grace a not-so-gentle shove. 'What are you waiting for? Get over there. This party's about to fold very soon anyway.'

Grace didn't need any further encouragement. Mitch was checking his watch and looking in her direction.

They exchanged cautious smiles and began to walk towards each other.

'Has anyone ever told you how stunning you look? How you stand out in a crowd?' he asked as they met.

'Thanks for the flowers, Mitch.'

He grinned and, heedless of curious stares, shot a possessive arm around her shoulders. 'That restaurant I men-

tioned last week,' he said, 'I have a booking for this evening. Will you join me for dinner?'

'Tonight?' She looked around at the scattered remaining
guests, the attendants now clearing away wine and food. A
waiter was chasing paper serviettes that had been caught
by a gust of sea air and now danced towards the pool. She
waved a hand at the scene. 'In the midst of all this, you
found time to make a booking?'

'And order flowers. That nosy little workmate of yours—
the one with the big mouth. She has her moments of efficiency.'

'Maria?' Grace felt her own mouth drop open and she
swung round to see Maria speeding through a side door.

'So you'll come?'

She couldn't bear to refuse. 'Is this point number three?'

His face broke into a slow, teasing smile. 'I didn't realise
you suffered from such a burning curiosity. Is this Pandora
complex of yours a new development?'

She suppressed a sigh, feeling on such tenterhooks, she
didn't know whether to laugh or cry. By accepting his flowers, by going out with Mitch, she was risking being hurt
one more time. Could she bear it if everything fell apart
now?

'Let's go,' Mitch urged.

She hesitated. 'Shouldn't I help with farewelling people?'

'No,' he answered succinctly. 'Maria and her crew are
doing a fine job.'

'What about George? I'm afraid I haven't looked after
him as well as you ordered.'

'George is fine. The Mayor's wife has invited him home
for dinner.'

'Oh, how nice,' murmured Grace. Her mouth opened

ready for another protest—but it was difficult to find something else to protest about.

With a finger pressed under her chin, Mitch nudged her lips together again. 'My beautiful Grace, forget George Hervey,' he whispered. 'Forget Maria. I want you to concentrate all your attention on me.'

Eyes brimming suddenly, she gave up and nodded her willingness.

He offered her his elbow. Obediently she threaded her arm through his, and together they hurried to the car park where Mitch's car waited.

They were the first diners to arrive at the old worker's cottage that had been restored and transformed into a restaurant. The sun was just setting as Grace and Mitch were led down a narrow brick path to the back garden.

A table in a secluded corner, under a spreading sea almond tree, was reserved for them. From the branches above hung bud lights fashioned into the shape of stars. Even though it wasn't completely dark, they looked very pretty, and Grace couldn't hide her delight.

'This is just lovely—quite enchanting,' she commented as soon as they were seated.

Mitch grinned. 'I thought it might be a little different.' He looked at her across the table and Grace knew from the appreciative glimmer in his eyes and the warmth of his smile that he was enjoying what he saw.

She wondered what they were going to talk about. Were they here, as she hoped, to build bridges?

'Do you realise this is our first official date?' Mitch asked.

'I guess so,' she answered softly, and his words increased her shyness. Carefully, she unfolded the starched serviette and spread it over her lap, wiping her damp palms as she did so.

He smiled. 'You know, with your tawny hair and natural tan, you make me think of a lioness—a proud and very lovely lioness.'

Grace had to smile. 'My star sign is Leo. Maybe that has something to do with it.'

'Leo? That would make your birthday some time soon, wouldn't it?'

'Yes,' she replied, feeling suddenly very awkward. 'August 6th, to be exact.'

A dark shadow dimmed Mitch's smile. 'The day you finish with the company,' he said softly.

'Life's full of little ironies,' she quipped, amazed at the steadiness in her voice.

The waiter arrived with a jug of iced water and the menus, and Grace was grateful for the distraction. She would be able to fill in some time choosing her meal. Now that she had the chance to fire questions at Mitch, to find out exactly where she stood, she was reluctant to probe.

The truth might hurt.

In the few minutes since they'd arrived, night had fallen and another group of diners entered the garden, chatting happily. Her eyes scanned the menu choices, and her hand flew to her mouth. Only one item was listed.

*Roasted freshwater crayfish and sautéed water lily bulbs served on a fresh pandanus leaf.*

Grace stared in silence at the page before her and her heart hammered loudly as she dragged her eyes past Mitch to the multiple loops of starry lights shimmering above them.

Her head spun.

'Grace, are you all right?' Mitch reached across the table and cupped her shaking hand in both of his.

She tried to speak, but she couldn't. *Crayfish, water lil-*

*ies, stars! What was going on here?* Tears welled, blurring her vision and blocking her throat.

'I know it's a bit theatrical of me,' Mitch said with a sheepish grin.

Grace managed to clear her throat. 'It certainly is,' she croaked, pointing to the menu and then to the stars above. 'Things like this are only supposed to happen in the movies.'

His fingers played with her hand. 'I wanted to find a way to take us back.'

'Back to the rock pool?'

'To when things were right between us.'

She watched as his strong brown fingers gently massaged her hand, while her heart jigged at a rickety pace. 'Out there...things...between us were very...*right*, weren't they?' she asked hesitantly.

'Couldn't have been *righter*.' He grinned, and Grace found it impossible not to smile back. He lifted her hand to his lips and her spine tingled deliciously as his mouth met her fingertips. 'When we were out there, we were able to forget about the outside world. We had no external pressures...'

'Apart from the pressure of survival,' Grace reminded him.

'Of course. And we shouldn't underestimate that we were in real danger. But, apart from that, the wilderness stripped us of all our emotional baggage, didn't it?'

Grace nodded. How could she not agree? She'd been a completely different person in the outback. So many times since they'd returned, she'd wondered if that had been the *real* Grace.

'We had no past, the future was in doubt, we had virtually no possessions,' he continued. 'We were just two people dealing with an ever-present danger. It's the kind of

situation that brings out the best and the worst in people.'
He squeezed her hand. 'And with us it was the best that
came out. The very best.'

'And the office brings out the worst?' She couldn't help
asking as she remembered how every time he'd tried to talk
to her lately they'd ended up fighting.

'I wouldn't say that,' Mitch replied thoughtfully. 'I think
what went wrong was the rapid transition back. We didn't
get a chance to adjust. When that army patrol turned up
out of the blue, everything finished so abruptly. One minute
we were about to make love, and the next we were winging
our way back to Townsville in a Black Hawk.'

She noticed that he didn't mention the minor detail of
Candy's intrusion into their lives.

'So what I propose,' he said, keeping her hand firmly in
his, 'is that tonight we try to cheat time.' Mitch's mouth
quirked into a crooked smile and Grace realised, with an
overwhelming rush of affection, that he was nervous. 'We
should imagine we are still at our outback rock pool, and
we can talk about how we want to continue from there. We
should forget about anything that has happened since then.'

Grace lowered her eyes from the intensity of his gaze.
'I'm leaving town, Mitch. How can we forget that I'm going away?'

'We just put it out of our minds for now.' He reached
out and snapped his fingers near her ear. 'Abracadabra.
We've gone back in time. Remember?'

'I'll try,' she whispered.

Mitch added, 'I think you'll find the crayfish and water
lilies are prepared in a more inventive manner than we
managed out in the bush.'

'I'm looking forward to it.' Grace sent him a newly determined and almost optimistic smile. 'And this restaurant
put on a special menu just for us?'

'Just for you and me, Grace. Consider yourself a celebrity.'

The meal was delicious. Mitch had already selected a very classy wine to accompany their food. The crayfish was served with a delicate pesto sauce and the water lilies were roasted with garlic and mushrooms. These were accompanied by a tasty side dish of carrots and green beans in a bush honey glaze.

While they ate, they carefully talked about the future as if there were no clouds on the horizon. They talked about *New Tomorrow*, about the location decisions, about how Mitch had first come up with the idea and what he hoped to achieve. It was all very pleasant.

Very safe.

But, while they waited for their desserts of exotic tropical fruit and ice cream drizzled with mango liqueur, Mitch reached out to take Grace's hand once more. He opened his mouth to speak and then seemed to lose confidence.

Surprised, she felt a sympathetic thrill bring goose bumps out on her arms. Even before Mitch spoke again, she knew he wanted to divert the conversation down a more serious path, and her heart began to pump painfully.

'Something happened to me in the outback,' he said at last, his dark eyes regarding her tenderly. 'It's never happened before.'

'Never?' she whispered.

He shook his head and his smile was actually shy. 'I've never fallen bang flat on my face into—into such emotional overload before.'

Their desserts arrived while Grace assimilated this admission.

Once the waiter had gone, she commented, 'This—this overload occurrence—doesn't sound like a very pleasant experience.'

Mitch put down his spoon. 'Grace, falling for you has to be the ultimate of all experiences I can expect in this lifetime.'

Her cheeks blazed.

'The painfully unpleasant part has been the aftermath. The way I made such a crazy mess of everything—and then received your resignation.'

She made a fuss of stirring her fruits into her ice cream while her mind and heart whizzed and thumped in dizzying confusion.

'All that stuff that's been written about unrequited love. It's actually worse than the poets make out.' While he spoke, Mitch switched to staring fiercely at the urn of ferns beside her, but now his eyes swung back to her. 'And I find it particularly painful when, deep down, I believe you really do care.'

Grace stabbed at her plate, but suddenly she couldn't see the fruit. 'You—' She gulped. 'That night in my flat, you said loving—I mean—being romantically attached to me—was inconvenient.'

'I said a lot of rubbish.'

'And what about…?'

His eyes speared hers. 'What about…what?'

Oh, why did she have so much difficulty asking questions…asking for kisses…asking about Candy…?

'Candy!' she burst out at last. 'What about Candy?' Her question seemed to hang in the air. And her heart beat so loudly, its sound filled her eardrums.

He frowned. 'Just what is it about Candy that has you so upset?'

Her mouth gaped. 'Everything!' she cried. Then she hurried on, 'No, if I'm honest, it's just one thing. The fact that you and she have a special *understanding*.'

'She told you that?'

Grace nodded. 'I couldn't stand thinking of you—of the two of you—'

'She claimed we were sleeping together?'

She shot him a challenging glare. 'She sure implied that.'

Mitch's fingers drummed on the tabletop. 'I can't believe you listened to her. How could you believe that?'

'Why shouldn't I?'

'Because I never gave you any reason to believe it.'

'Oh?' Grace gulped. She could think of several times Mitch had allowed Candy to drape herself all over him. Several days he'd spent closeted with her in his office. Several nights he'd spent in the same hotel as her.

Still, she had to admit, there was no real evidence.

'I didn't touch the woman. Yeah, she made a play for me, but I don't think I even gave her a peck on the cheek. I swear it.' His thoughtful gaze held hers, but then dropped as he picked up his wineglass and carefully placed it at another spot on the table, as if he were moving a chess piece. He stared at the glass as he spoke. 'You know she made it a condition of the finance that I get rid of you?'

'What?' The blood rushed into Grace's cheeks.

'I wouldn't hear of it, of course.'

'But, Mitch, you could have lost everything.'

*Lost everything!*

His company, his project, his dreams! *Everything!* Stunned, Grace stared at him, her own words echoing over and over in her head. He would have sacrificed all that *for her*!

'I couldn't let you go.'

'Oh, no,' groaned Grace. 'And then I resigned anyhow.' Her guilty eyes grew round as another thought struck. 'That night I resigned...you wanted me to come back to dinner at the hotel, hoping I'd suss Candy out and—and find a way to support you.'

Grace couldn't bear thinking about how she'd let Mitch down, how she'd roared out of that car park without giving him a chance to explain, how she'd handed in that primly worded, watertight resignation…had refused to talk…

His soft words broke through her remorse. 'We've got to forget all that now. All I want to think about tonight is you, my sweet girl. About us. Ever since we got back to town, it's been like there was a part of me that was missing. The most vital part.'

His astonishing words flowed into her, bringing with them a flood of warmth and well-being. 'I've been an absolute mess, too,' she whispered, and her admission seemed to set something free inside her. It was as if all the pieces of her disintegrating heart were being drawn together and were settling back into place.

'Let's get out of here,' urged Mitch, scraping back his chair as he jumped to his feet. 'We have some serious catching up to do.'

The waiter was approaching their table with a tray holding coffee and chocolates. Mitch quickly explained that they were leaving and asked for the bill instead and, as soon as he had dealt with it, he bundled Grace ahead of him out of the restaurant. His car was parked only a few metres away.

'Now, where was I?' he murmured, gathering her into his arms as he leaned back against the car door, pulling her with him.

'You were going to kiss me?' she asked breathlessly.

'Just a moment,' he teased in a throaty whisper. His lips moved slowly up her neck to linger along her jawline. 'It' my turn to ask for a kiss.'

In a sensuous haze, she lifted her arms to circle his neck. Slowly, she repeated his action, moving her lips along his

aw and nibbling gently. 'You can start asking any time
ou like.'

As kisses went, it eclipsed all the others. Shameless de-
ire ricocheted through Grace with the lightning pace of a
aser. In seconds she was trembling with need. 'Take me
ome quickly, Mitch,' she pleaded.

'Try stopping me.'

They reached her flat in record time and tumbled out of
he car in a laughing, eager scurry. Mitch kissed her again
t the front door and, once inside, he clasped her to him
vith a groan of raw passion.

'Grace, you've no idea…'

'Shush,' she whispered against his cheek and, taking him
y the hand, she led him across her lounge room.

'Hold on, sweetheart.' His arms came round her, halting
er progress. He held her against him and lifted her hair
way from her face, tucking it behind one ear. 'Any minute
ow I'm going to totally lose my head, but there's some-
ing I want to say first.' He kissed her exposed ear, then
miled at her.

By the soft light of a table-lamp, she could see the tender
varmth in his eyes, the slight tremor at the corner of his
outh. Her heart sky-rocketed.

'I need to tell you about…' he murmured roughly, but
en his words died as his lips grazed hers, once, twice,
nd with his body he steered her to the sofa. He pulled her
own beside him for a kiss that was deep and hungry and
rgent—as if he needed her more than oxygen.

And, when he finally pulled away, she cried, 'Don't
op!'

'I thought you wanted to know about points four and
ve.'

'I thought you'd started.'

Her eyes were held by his suddenly serious expression.

'Not quite.' He held her close and ordered softly, 'M:
Robbins, I'm going to explain these points very clearly and
I will expect you to take in every detail.'

Taking her hands in his, he stroked with his thumbs the
faint blue veins just beneath the skin of her wrists. 'First
don't ever let anything or anyone like Candy get in ou
way again.'

She nodded, and sobbed happy tears. 'I'm sorry, Mitch
I was too willing to misjudge you. I was so sure you were
prepared to do anything to achieve business success.'

'What you must realise is that I love you, Grace,' he said
softly, just a little shyly. 'And this is a first for me. I've
never felt this way about anybody. I love your mind, you
body—every tiny, wonderful thing about—'

She couldn't resist throwing her arms about his neck and
crushing his lips with hers. 'Oh, Mitch,' she cried. 'Oh
Mitch. I'm so happy. I can't believe this.'

'You'd better believe it,' he said, pressing a warning fin
ger to her mouth. 'And you must promise me that you
won't be afraid to ask me anything. Come to me with every
doubt. I—I want to share my life with you.'

Tears poured down Grace's cheeks and burned he
throat. She couldn't speak, but she leaned her face against
his and kissed Mitch with happy little kisses.

His hands came up to cradle her head and he returned
her kiss with breathtaking reverence. When at last he lifted
his face from hers, he smiled. 'I'm afraid I can't promise
you wealth. Tropicana Films might end up successful, bu
that's in the lap of the gods at this stage. All I can offe
you is my love and my life, but I am hoping that will be
enough to convince you that we should be married.'

She swiped at her tears and smiled through her sniffles

'So this is my fourth point. Will you marry me?'

'I have a point to make, too.'

'You'll marry me?'

'Just a minute, Mitch,' she said gently. 'Now you're the impatient one.'

'No doubt about that. Come on, put me out of my misery.'

'I just want to make it clear that I love you too, Mitch. I'm sorry for the kind of tantrums that prompted me to resign. I want to tell you I'd stay here to be with you without the job. I might love my work, but I know now that I love you more.'

'Thank God,' breathed Mitch. 'But you've kind of stolen my thunder. The last point I planned to demand was that a condition of our marriage involved throwing that resignation out the window. Do you think you could handle having me as your boss and your husband?'

'I actually think we make a pretty good team.' Grace knew her smile was a mile wide.

'Unless, of course, you want to get straight into babies and all that scene,' Mitch hastily corrected.

Grace snuggled up close to her man—her sweet gentleman disguised as a seriously sexy, A-grade hunk. 'I'll tell you exactly what I want, Mr W.' She looked him straight in the eye as she spoke. 'I want to make love with you, and I want to marry you, Mitch, my darling. And in between I want to work with you and make movies with you and, one day in the future, I want to make babies with you.' She ticked off her five fingers as she made each point. 'That's the order I have in mind. How does it sound to you?'

Mitch lined his hand up with hers, palm to palm, finger to finger. 'That sounds like the perfect five-point plan to me.'

EPILOGUE

# *BIG NIGHT AT THE OSCARS FOR AUSSIES*

**Glamour abounded at this year's Oscars; however, *MOVIE MAG'S* Bridget Winter reports that the Australian contingent from *New Tomorrow* stole the show.**

Waiting fans, who had already seen quite a few celebrities make their way down the famous red carpet, erupted when Mitch Wentworth arrived. Tall and rugged in a sleek Armani tuxedo, Mitch looked more like a film star than the producer-director of *New Tomorrow*.

Arm in arm with Mitch was his truly radiant wife of three years, Grace Robbins, and she looked totally stunning in a sea-green body net dusted with seed-pearls. Most of the media contingent agreed that her outfit was by far the most arresting and attractive of the evening.

In fact, Mitch and Grace stole the spotlight from the stars.

Grace's gown will be auctioned to raise money for charity, and bidding is expected to reach tens of thousands.

But the most excited and confused man in the Dorothy Chandler Pavilion was surprise Oscar winner Henry Aspinall, who has been flooded with offers from other Hollywood movie-makers since scoring his award for Most Creative Use of New Technology.

During his emotional acceptance speech, Henry paid tribute to his boss, Mitch Wentworth, thanking him for seeing the amazing potential in his original computer graphics.

Looking like an absent-minded professor who'd stumbled into the Awards Night by mistake, Henry had a permanent attachment in the form of High Sierra's ever-present Candy Sorbell.

After the huge box office success of *New Tomorrow*, Wentworth and crew are now filming a romance set in Thailand from a script written by his talented wife.

Hollywood rumour says these two are inseparable, and it seems that working side by side must agree with them. Grace and Mitch Wentworth have that very special aura which suggests they enjoy the kind of happily ever after the rest of us usually only find at the movies.

# THE AUSTRALIANS

## MEN WHO TURN YOUR WHOLE WORLD UPSIDE DOWN!

Look out for novels about the Wonder from Down Under—where spirited women win the hearts of Australia's most eligible men.

Harlequin Romance®:

**OUTBACK WITH THE BOSS**
Barbara Hannay (September, #3670)

**MASTER OF MARAMBA**
Margaret Way (October, #3671)

**OUTBACK FIRE**
Margaret Way (December, #3678)

Harlequin Presents®:

**A QUESTION OF MARRIAGE**
Lindsay Armstrong (October, #2208)

**FUGITIVE BRIDE**
Miranda Lee (November, #2212)

*Available wherever Harlequin books are sold.*

HARLEQUIN®
*Makes any time special* ®

*Harlequin truly does*
*make any time special....*
*This year we are celebrating*
*weddings in style!*

To help us celebrate, we want you to tell us how wearing the Harlequin wedding gown will make your wedding day special. As the grand prize, Harlequin will offer one lucky bride the chance to **"Walk Down the Aisle" in the Harlequin wedding gown!**

### There's more...

For her honeymoon, she and her groom will spend five nights at the **Hyatt Regency Maui.** As part of this five-night honeymoon at the hotel renowned for its romantic attractions, the couple will enjoy a candlelit dinner for two in Swan Court, a sunset sail on the hotel's catamaran, and duet spa treatments.

A HYATT RESORT AND SPA

Maui • Molokai • Lanai

To enter, please write, in, 250 words or less, how wearing the Harlequin wedding gown will make your wedding day special. The entry will be judged based on its emotionally compelling nature, its originality and creativity, and its sincerity. This contest is open to Canadian and U.S. residents only and to those who are 18 years of age and older. There is no purchase necessary to enter. Void where prohibited. See further contest rules attached. Please send your entry to:

### Walk Down the Aisle Contest

| In Canada | In U.S.A. |
|---|---|
| P.O. Box 637 | P.O. Box 9076 |
| Fort Erie, Ontario | 3010 Walden Ave. |
| L2A 5X3 | Buffalo, NY 14269-9076 |

You can also enter by visiting www.eHarlequin.com
***Win the Harlequin wedding gown and the vacation of a lifetime!***
The deadline for entries is October 1, 2001.

**HARLEQUIN®**
*Makes any time special ®*

If you enjoyed what you just read,
then we've got an offer you can't resist!

# Take 2 bestselling
# love stories FREE!
# Plus get a FREE surprise gift!

**Clip this page and mail it to Harlequin Reader Service®**

| IN U.S.A. | IN CANADA |
|---|---|
| 3010 Walden Ave. | P.O. Box 609 |
| P.O. Box 1867 | Fort Erie, Ontario |
| Buffalo, N.Y. 14240-1867 | L2A 5X3 |

**YES!** Please send me 2 free Harlequin Romance® novels and my free surprise gift. After receiving them, if I don't wish to receive anymore, I can return the shipping statement marked cancel. If I don't cancel, I will receive 6 brand-new novels every month, before they're available in stores! In the U.S.A., bill me at the bargain price of $3.15 plus 25¢ shipping & handling per book and applicable sales tax, if any*. In Canada, bill me at the bargain price of $3.59 plus 25¢ shipping & handling per book and applicable taxes**. That's the complete price and a savings of 10% off the cover prices—what a great deal! I understand that accepting the 2 free books and gift places me under no obligation ever to buy any books. I can always return a shipment and cancel at any time. Even if I never buy another book from Harlequin, the 2 free books and gift are mine to keep forever.

186 HEN DC7K
386 HEN DC7L

| Name | | (PLEASE PRINT) | |
|---|---|---|---|
| Address | | Apt.# | |
| City | | State/Prov. | Zip/Postal Code |

\* Terms and prices subject to change without notice. Sales tax applicable in N.Y.
\*\* Canadian residents will be charged applicable provincial taxes and GST.
All orders subject to approval. Offer limited to one per household and not valid to current Harlequin Romance® subscribers.
® are registered trademarks of Harlequin Enterprises Limited.

HROM01                                    ©2001 Harlequin Enterprises Limited

# COMING SOON...

**AN EXCITING
OPPORTUNITY TO SAVE
ON THE PURCHASE OF
HARLEQUIN AND
SILHOUETTE BOOKS!**

*DETAILS TO FOLLOW
IN OCTOBER 2001!*

*YOU WON'T WANT TO MISS IT!*

PHQ401